the past can wait

Cheryl Burman

This is a work of fiction. Names, characters, businesses, places, events, locales, and incidents are either the products of the author's imagination or used in a fictitious manner. Any resemblance to actual persons, living or dead, or actual events is purely coincidental.

First published in the UK in 2024 by Holborn House Ltd

©2024 Cheryl Burman

Apart from any use permitted under UK copyright law, this publication may only be reproduced, stored, or transmitted, in any form, or by any means, with the prior permission in writing of the publishers or, in the case of reprographic production, in accordance with the terms and licences issued by the Copyright Licensing Agency.

By Cheryl Burman

For grownups

NOVELS

Keepers

Book two *Walking in the Rain*

Book three *The Past can Wait*

River Witch

COLLECTED SHORT STORIES

Dragon Gift: ten short stories

Who can believe in witches? and other stories

For big and little kids of any age

GUARDIANS OF THE FOREST TRILOGY

Book one *The Wild Army*

Book two *Quests*

Book three *Gryphon Magic*

Prequel *Legend of the Winged Lion*

Sequel *Winter of the White Horde*

www.cherylburman.com

Foreword

The final scenes of *Keepers* and much of *Walking in the Rain* are set in the Australian Snowy Mountains early in the days of the gargantuan Snowy Mountains Hydro-Electric Scheme. The Scheme also provides the backdrop to a significant part of *The Past can Wait*. While I have given brief explanations where they would occur naturally, some readers might like to know more about this amazing engineering feat which took some twenty-five years to construct and turned rivers around, all to provide water to Australia's dry hinterland. You can read about it on my website – search on the bottom bar for Snowy Mountains Scheme.

I also need to say that the bare facts of The Snowy Mountains Authority buying out the graziers and moving the town of Adaminaby to make way for Lake Eucumbene are correct. However, the manner in which the Authority undertook this, eg delaying payments and other aspects as described in this novel, are purely from my imagination.

Chapter One

WHEN IT'S 110° OUTSIDE, COOLNESS is relative. Maggie has little to be grateful for today, except the non-stifling air in the darkened wards. The Royal's old, thick bluestone walls, and the blinds drawn to battle the midday sun's stabbing rays help the illusion.

In the two rows of metal beds divided by a wide corridor, heat affected and sickness-drowsy patients lie under loose sheets. Jugs of water on bedside tables are constantly refilled, the sufferers urged to drink. A doctor at the end of the ward rolls up his sleeves as he talks to a nurse who jots notes on a patient's chart.

Maggie returns from the nurses' station to set a vase of yellow roses on the wide window sill by Mrs Harrington's bed. The old lady is sitting up with the thin straps of her summer nightgown revealing sunspot-scattered skin stretched like parchment across her bony collarbone.

Shifting a rose to the left, Maggie tilts her head to see the effect. 'Hmm,' she says. 'Flower arranging, sadly, isn't taught in nursing school.' Today, even this vibrant colour fails to cheer her. The roses must sense her bitter turmoil.

Mrs Harrington rests her magazine on her knees. 'I've told the children not to bring flowers. It makes more work for you nurses, and I'm sorry.'

Maggie leaves the roses to do what they will. 'Nonsense,' she says. 'Without flowers,' with a cheery wave at the vase, 'the wards would be pretty dull, hey?' Mrs Harrington doesn't deserve Maggie's misery inflicted on her.

Her patient grins. 'You always see the best in things, Nurse Greene.'

'Ah, yes, I try to.' Maggie gulps down grief, lets her gaze drop briefly to her white shoes. Pretending efficiency, she gives the sheet crumpled across Mrs Harrington's bony lap a straightening tug. 'Can I get you something? A tea?'

'Oh no, dear. Far too hot for tea.' Mrs Harrington nods

at the water jug. 'This will do.'

Maggie pours a glass and offers it. As Mrs Harrington carefully takes the water from Maggie's hand, vertical frown lines crisscross the horizontal ones on her pale, wrinkled forehead.

'Is everything all right, dear?' She gives Maggie a quick upward glance.

Maggie's eyes well at the old lady's perception and at the offered sympathy. She blinks. 'Thank you, Mrs H, everything is fine,' she lies. She fumbles for the watch pinned to her uniform, needing an excuse to not catch that worried gaze. Those knowing eyes will be Maggie's undoing, and crying on duty is a humiliation she wishes to avoid.

'Now,' she says, forcing a false brightness, 'I have a ward full of other patients to see to. I'll check in with you later.'

She walks off briskly, her soft white nurses' shoes squeaking on the polished linoleum floor. Brushing at her unwanted tears, Maggie heads towards Mrs Cooper. The woman's constant carping about the food, the doctors, the weather, her lack of visitors, will banish Maggie's self-pity in a heartbeat.

There's no time, however, to brood on the events of New Year's Eve's party. The extreme hot weather on this second day of January 1955 brings a slew of heat-exhausted young and elderly. Maggie and her colleagues peel off patients' clothing, bathe parched skin in cool water, and ensure those in their care drink frequently. She and her colleagues move rapidly from one victim to the other, coping with this addition to their workload.

After several hours, a lull in admissions allows Maggie to seek refuge in the hospital canteen. Despite the drawn blinds, the heat of the blazing late afternoon sun forces its way into the room. Red-faced patients, staff and visitors slump at tables like wilted vegetables, listlessly fanning themselves with limp newspapers and magazines. Fractious children whine at their mothers' knees. It's hardly the cool

The Past can Wait

quiet Maggie craves.

Sweaty, footsore, her uniform crumpled like she's worn it for a week, Maggie is too tired to decide whether she most needs a drink to quench her burning thirst, or food to feed her hollow stomach. Armed with a pot of tea and a cheese and tomato sandwich dried out by the sticky air, she eases herself into a chair at a corner table, sets down the tray, and rests her head in her hands.

'Maggie.'

The voice brings Maggie's head up. She stares at her friend and fellow nurse – and hostess of the disastrous party.

'June.' Maggie wrinkles her nose, comparing June's neatly pinned cap sitting pertly on her blonde curls, her blue and white uniform crisply perfect. 'How's your day going?'

'Busy. This heat …' June pulls out a chair, reaching across to lay a cool hand on Maggie's damp arm. 'I've been hoping to come across you.' Her blue gaze peers into Maggie's weary eyes. 'I've been worried ever since the party. You were so upset when you left, and Alf tells me Arthur's gone back to Adaminaby already. What's happened?'

Already? Maggie looks away. Exhaustion exaggerates her fraught emotions, and she no more wants to have a crying fit in the busy canteen than she did in the ward. 'Arthur and me … we've …' She swallows. 'We've broken off the engagement.'

'No! You can't have. Not you and Arthur.'

Maggie's face crumples at June's genuine horror. She pulls a handkerchief from her pinafore pocket and dabs at her eyes.

'Why?' June says. 'The two of you are the perfect couple. At least, it seemed like it to me.'

Maggie lets out a long, ragged breath, determined not to let the tears fall. '*Were* the perfect couple.' She bites her trembling lower lip. 'Do you know how long Arthur and me have been together?'

June blinks at the belligerent tone.

'Five bloody years.' Maggie places her clasped hands on the table, pushing aside the uneaten sandwich. 'Five years of promises, and no delivering.' She uses the hankie to wipe perspiration from her forehead. 'At your party, we were talking about how well Dad's doing after his heart attack last year, how he can go to work some days, or help Teddy in the shop, which means Mum doesn't need me at home anymore, and we can marry as soon as we can organise it—' she pauses, feeling the pain of what came after '— and he tells me ... he tells me ...' A gulp of breath and an injection of disappointed fury into her voice. 'He wants us to move to that God-forsaken township in the mountains.'

'Cooma?' June's defences come up at the mention of her home town. 'It's not the city, nothing like here. The old place has its charms though, and—'

Maggie hastens to explain. 'Not Cooma. Maybe, possibly, I could think about there.'

It's not been more than a few months since June left Cooma and the Snowy Mountains to marry Alf. As a fellow nurse and the sister of Alf's oldest friend, it naturally befell Maggie to make sure June settled in. She found the task easy, and not only because of her own outgoing, some would say ebullient, nature. Maggie admires the way the practical, calm June has adapted to the city, yet she understands her new friend must miss her quieter, rural life.

June relaxes. 'You mean Adaminaby?'

Maggie rolls her eyes. 'Yes. The *village* with the unpronounceable name where the Authority bases itself.'

When Arthur took a management job with the Snowy Mountains Authority in Adaminaby, Maggie made a rare visit to the library and read up on Adaminaby's short history.

'When it was a gold mining town it was barely worth the name,' she snaps. 'And it's not much bigger these days, is it?' Maggie challenges June to tell her Adaminaby has improved out of sight since becoming the centre for the huge hydro-electric construction scheme currently reshaping much of the Snowy Mountains.

June taps her chin. 'Not as far as I know. There's no reason to do anything there until they move it all. You've heard about the flooding?'

Maggie throws out her hands. 'Exactly. Last year Arthur talked about how the buildings, and the people, have to be moved, because their great new dam will flood it all.' She narrows her eyes. 'Great place to start married life.'

'I agree,' June says, 'so why on earth go there? I thought the idea was for Arthur to bring in a lot of money quickly and, with you working too, buy a house here. One of the shiny all mod cons ones Alf's helping to build in these new suburbs.' She grins. 'Like my house.'

Maggie pictures June's red brick single storey home on the coast not far south of the city. The neat building is set back from a quiet crescent on a large block of land. Similar red or cream houses fill the former sheep paddocks around it to create a new community. Yes, she wants a home like June's.

'Yeah.' Maggie sips her cooling tea. 'Me too. But Arthur's had promotions, landed himself a management job. Means more money. Good. Also means he's more interested in staying. Bad.' She pouts. 'Great prospects, Maggie, he tells me, deadly serious. Cheap living, and we can save for our house together …' She groans. 'No thank you very much.'

'So it's all off? After five years?' June's frown returns. 'I haven't known you long, Maggie, and I hardly know Arthur at all, given he's up in the mountains …' Her understanding smile threatens to re-awaken Maggie's tears. 'I will say though, I can recognise the extra bounce in your step when he's in town. Are you sure that's what you want to do?'

Maggie gulps the last of her tea and stands. She slides the untouched sandwich towards June. 'Here, you have it. I can't stomach food today.'

'And?' June persists with her question.

Maggie puffs a dismissive breath and lifts her arms to settle her awry cap more firmly on her springy dark curls. 'I love him, June. But I'm not prepared to abandon my life, my job, my family to drag myself up there.' She drops her arms and presses her palms to the table, peering intently at her friend. 'Remember, I abandoned a life once, when we came here to Australia after the war. That was good, because what we left behind was rubbish – literally, bombed-out East End rubbish.'

'It wouldn't be forever, right?'

Maggie snorts. 'The way Arthur talks about it, it could be.' She straightens, waves her hand. 'It's good here when it's not so damn hot. It's my home. Arthur's not offering me better prospects. He's offering me a different kind of rubbish.' She glances at the big clock on the wall. 'Gotta go, patients needing their meds. See you soon, love to Alfie.'

She leaves June sitting with more to be said, Maggie guesses, and strides off between the tables, dodging children playing hide-and-seek on the floor and patients and visitors carrying trays of drinks and food. June's troubled gaze warms her back like firelight on a cold night.

Chapter Two

THERE'S TOO MUCH TIME TO think on a train, and then a bus. Normally, Arthur takes the night train to Melbourne, tries to sleep. He won't sleep this time, hasn't slept since the party, which is why he's travelling by day, hoping the views will distract him.

Through the train window's grimy glass, a herd of kangaroos bound across the cracked, brown earth. Something must have spooked them because it's too hot even for 'roos to move fast. Arthur squints, searching for signs of a fire. There's nothing bar flatness intersected with barbed wire fencing and an occasional tree sending a long shadow in the early evening light. He looks forward to the hillier, although no greener, landscape nearer Melbourne. Mostly he looks forward to the long journey's end.

This day time travelling is more than about distraction. It's a lot to do with not hanging about the city any longer than he has to. He can't face his and Maggie's friends right now. Teddy, Maggie's brother, will be furious with him, not bothering to consider it isn't Arthur's idea to break up. Raine, Teddy's wife, will be hurt on Maggie's behalf. As for Alf … Thank God he and June have a telephone, which means Arthur didn't have to go to their home to tell them in person he was leaving earlier than expected, and wouldn't make their planned outing to see the newly released 'Rear Window'. It was still a difficult conversation.

'Pity,' Alf said. 'Work emergency?'

'No.' Arthur tugged at the telephone cord in the public phone box, breathing in the scent of the bodies which had gone before. He was tempted to make up an emergency, except the truth would come out quickly, so why lie to his best friend? 'It's, well …' He couldn't say it, because if he said the words out loud – me and Maggie aren't engaged anymore – they would take on a reality Arthur wasn't ready to face. If he ever would be. He fudged, blurred the truth to match the blurred heaviness in his head. And his heart. 'Need to get my head straight on some things, need time to myself.'

'Ah.'

Arthur sent a silent, desperate plea into the black mouthpiece. Please don't ask if you can help, mate. 'I'll be in touch,' he blurted. 'Say hi to June.' And he hung up.

It will be out by this time. Maggie will see June at work, thick as thieves those two, and spill all. It's true what Arthur said to Alf. He needs time to think things through. Starting with Maggie's accusations, which rewind in his head day and night.

It began as a regular conversation at the New Year party, about Maggie's mum pushing her to set a wedding date. This time, Maggie didn't mock her mother like she normally did. She pushed too.

'Not yet.' Arthur rubbed his short beard, wishing he'd thought to shave it before coming down from the cooler mountains to the hot city. 'A bit longer. I mean, we planned to wait to afford a house, have a home of our own to raise our kids, a roof forever over our heads.' He clasped her gently by the shoulders. 'It's what we both want, always has been.'

Maggie shifted her gaze to stare over his shoulder into the shadows of the moonlit garden. The shrill cacophony of crickets fought against laughter and the bass thrum of music from inside the house.

'I know why you so badly want it, Arthur, I do.'

Maggie wriggled out of his grasp and placed a warm hand on his arm. He wanted to cover the hand with his own, draw her close, not let go.

'You've told me, and I thought I understood,' she murmured. 'But now … Well, these days it's an obsession. An unhealthy one.'

Yes, he'd told her. The day after Teddy's 21st birthday party back in 1949. The end of a long, fun evening, the

The Past can Wait

few remaining guests lounging about on the floor and the sofas in the camp's Nissen hut, the talk desultory. Someone mentioned the Snowy Mountains Scheme, saying it had been launched that day. Arthur, and their Italian friend, Sep, had said they'd like to go, save a lot of money in a short time and be set for life, or for a good part of life at least.

My birthday present, to amuse me, Teddy had joked, while claiming anyone who went there to tunnel into mountains, live in tents in the cold and snow, would have to be mad.

'Then I'm mad,' Arthur said to Maggie the next evening. He'd asked her out to see a film, just the two of them. Afterwards, strolling over the river along King William Road to the bus stop in a mild spring warmth, he took up the conversation which had been playing in his mind all day. 'A bloke could save enough to buy a house.' He was pleased at the glint in her dark eyes.

'You could. Wouldn't take long to put together a deposit.'

'No.' Arthur shook his head. 'I mean enough to buy outright, own it, nothing they could take from you.' He'd expected the straightforward Maggie to ask questions about the bitter edge to his voice. She didn't. She frowned, murmured good idea, and talked about the film.

It wasn't until much later, the night he asked her to marry him, that he spoke of all of it, of what drives him to want the permanency of ownership.

The train arrives at Spencer Street. Arthur hauls his cardboard suitcase from the rack and follows other passengers onto the platform. It's as hot here as it is at home, the setting sun bringing little relief. He'll stay at the same small hotel he always does. The rooms are clean and cheap, the chenille bed covers are worn, and the middle-aged, mousy receptionist stares through him, pretending she hasn't seen him four times a year for the last five years. Arthur likes the anonymity.

He sleeps better than expected, worn out at last, and

groggily wakes to fumble the jangle of his travel clock – a leather-encased present from Maggie last Christmas. After a breakfast of bacon, eggs and fried tomatoes in an early opening café near the bus station, he buys his ticket, sees his case stowed in the belly of the elderly coach, and takes a seat by a window.

The winding, day-long journey is eternal, the brief stops an irritation. And every mile is marked by Maggie's words from the party looping in his skull.

'Enough is enough,' she said. 'Who in their right mind waits until they can pay for a house in cash?' She threw out her hands. 'Certainly not the likes of us.'

'I can't give it up.' To give up at this stage, when he's so close, would be to waste the years before. 'I've told you why.'

'Old history, Arthur.' Maggie faced him with a ferocity which welling tears couldn't soften. 'What happened to your family … I get it, but you can't keep hanging on to the past.' She swallowed the tears, glared. 'Don't you want us to be together?'

'Of course,' he cried. Which was when the solution hit him. He grinned, grasped her arms. 'Come up there with me. We can be married, move to the mountains.'

Maggie blinked, frowned.

Arthur pushed on, thrilled with his plan. 'We'll have somewhere to live, cheap. We can save, and in a few years, come home–'

'Move to the mountains?' Maggie wriggled out of his grasp, her hands waving at waist level in denial. 'To the back of beyond?' Her voice rose on the last word. 'To the one-horse town not worthy of the name?' She stared at him, her mouth forming a gaping O like he'd suggested they go live in the Congo in a mud hut.

Arthur didn't understand. It was the perfect compromise. 'Beautiful scenery, great prospects.' In his haste to persuade her, he sounded like one of those government posters they used in England to tempt families to emigrate to Australia. 'The people are friendly,' he insisted, eager for her to believe how friendly everyone is. 'You'd love it. This way we can work together for our dream.'

'Your dream, Arthur.' Maggie stood, unmoving. Sweat gleamed on her forehead. 'I wouldn't love it, and if that's how well you know me – to think I'd give up my life here, my family, my nursing – to traipse after you to the middle of nowhere …' She pulled in her lips. 'It's always about what you think is best, isn't it?' she said, and he didn't recognise the acid in her tone. 'You never ask me what I think.'

'I never ask you?' Arthur's confusion deepened. Hadn't they agreed this together? 'What–'

'When you took the office job, committed to staying up there longer…' Maggie's voice rose, rushing the words. 'You told me about it after you'd accepted, never occurred to you to see if I agreed with the idea, was I willing to hang about longer.' She crossed her arms. The moonlight caught the angry glint in her eyes. 'Did it?'

'I didn't think–'

'Exactly!'

'I'm sorry, Maggie.' Arthur reached out his arms. Maggie stepped away, and he dropped them to his side. 'Don't you see?' He desperately wanted her – this woman who would be his wife, whom he loved – to realise the sense of his idea. 'Don't you see, we can do both? Be together *and* have our home?'

Pearly tears glistened on her cheeks. He wanted to reach up to pat the tears dry. He hated upsetting her.

'No, I don't.' Maggie wove her fingers together, glanced at him with eyes full of pain. 'I've had enough, Arthur.' Her voice quivered.

Sitting in the hot bus, his sweat-damp trousers clinging to his skin, Arthur drops his head into his hands and relives the nightmare vision of Maggie tugging at her finger, yanking off the ring they'd bought together at the fancy jeweller in Regent's Arcade. She handed it to him on her open, shaking palm, and he took it, a reflex, and then she swung on her high heels and strode into the house. Her shoulders heaved.

'Maggie, wait.' He'd clutched the ring so tightly the small diamond cut into his palm. When she didn't stop, he strode after her, and he would have caught her, except as he reached the crowded living room, the shouted countdown to midnight reached zero. Arthur was swept up in a tangle of drunken hugs and happy new years. By the time he squeezed his way out of the house, Maggie was gone.

The old coach grunts its snail pace across paddocks rich with purple-hued Paterson's Curse, or ploughed brown, furrowed for seeding, until they reach the mountains where cattle and sheep graze undulating plains rising to tall peaks. Finally, the coach shudders to a grateful stop at the station in Cooma.

Two youngsters scramble to the door in a clamour of shouting about seeing daddy while their mother stretches to pull bags from the shelf. Arthur helps her, receives a grateful thanks, and follows her off the coach.

The evening is mild, fresh-washed with rain as evidenced by the puddles he skirts on his way to the hotel where he'll stay the night. Bone weary, hungry, and heartsore, Arthur breathes in the sweetness, searching for comfort, even if it's only air. He hopes he's not too late to grab a bite in the dining room. With luck, he's exhausted enough to earn another decent night's sleep before the final leg by local bus to Adaminaby.

It's good he's returned early, he tells himself, because with the moving of the town and the opening of the first power station in the Scheme next month, there's a pile of work mounting on his desk. The power station is at Guthega, where Teddy worked for a few months when he was hiding out from Raine. Arthur should invite Teddy to visit for the big ceremony. He cracks a smile, the first since New Year's

Eve, imagining Teddy's scathing response. His friend never was a fan of the mountains, his pronouncement that you had to be mad to come here reinforced by nearly dying in a showdown with a frontloader on a treed, snowy slope.

Arthur pushes open the door of the Australia Hotel and is greeted by the familiar odour of beery carpet and furniture polish. And his name called across from the doorway of the Ladies' Lounge.

'Arthur? Is that you?'

He turns to the voice, attracted by its undertone of bubbling mirth. The owner is willowy, with waves of auburn hair to her bare shoulders and a wide smile. She doesn't wait for his recognition.

'Alf's friend, right?' The woman walks swiftly up to him, slaps a manicured hand to her chest. 'It's me, Libby, remember? I met you when you visited Alf one time.' Libby's glittering beam suggests meeting Arthur is what she's been waiting for all evening, possibly her whole life. 'Happy new year!'

Chapter Three

MAGGIE LAYS HER GEORGETTE HEYER novel face down on the table in the hospital canteen and takes a mouthful of tepid tea. She has no idea what's going on with Miss Heyer's current feisty heroine. Her desolate mind is far away. In fact, Maggie's not taking in much of anything these days, although she works hard at hiding her heartache from family and colleagues.

'It'll take time,' June counselled her in the days after the breakup with Arthur. 'Or you can tell him you didn't mean what you said, you were too hasty, caught by surprise, and–'

Maggie had pushed her empty lemonade glass across June's kitchen table. 'Do what Raine did?' Her lips twitched at the memory of her spirited, pint-sized sister-in-law, eight months pregnant, dragging a reluctant Alf to the mountains to search for her absent husband, Teddy. Teddy might be Maggie's younger brother but Maggie firmly believes he has the better part of that marriage.

June didn't laugh. She'd been there when the drama cracked wide open, with Teddy at death's door and Raine going into early labour with their daughter. It was how June and Alf met.

'You could,' June said. 'Depends what you want. To have Arthur back–'

'And be stuck in the bush for years to come?' Maggie crossed her arms. 'No. I don't care how much it hurts, which is a lot. There's no way I'm crawling on hands and knees, begging forgiveness for what's not my fault.'

Which doesn't stop her thinking a hundred times a day what Arthur is feeling. Is he sorry, is he hurting too? Will he come home, confess to being in the wrong and … She breathes out a short huff and picks up the book, praying for distraction.

'Mind if I sit here?'

A tall, young doctor smiles above Maggie. Her brow

The Past can Wait

puckers. Bar the necessary interactions in the workplace, Dr Elliott hasn't spoken to her since she firmly rebuffed his keen advances about a year before.

At the time, she'd waved her engagement ring in his direction, explaining tartly that whatever his morals were, hers insisted on fidelity to the man she was promised to. He grinned and wandered off, his careless shrug briefly making Maggie's blood boil.

Dark brown wavy hair a mite too long to flop endearingly in his velvet brown eyes, an aquiline nose and sophisticated charm, make Luke Elliott a favourite among the nurses. He doesn't need to bother about those who refuse to fawn at his feet.

Maggie has no desire for the doctor's company. With exaggerated care, she moves her head to take in the sparsely populated canteen. Visiting hours are over, patients in their beds eating their evening meals. A handful of staff are left, sitting singly or in pairs, resting before returning to work. Her survey is pointed. Why interrupt *her*?

Dr Elliott ignores the message. He's taken her silence for agreement and has set a thick white plate containing a sandwich on the table.

Maggie gives in. Summoning energy to send him on his way is beyond her. 'Help yourself,' she says with an edge of sarcasm. She shuffles her chair further into the corner, distancing herself from the one he pulls out. She bends to her book, irritated, and determined to find its pages compulsive.

'Hot today. As ever.' The doctor seats himself and lifts the sandwich, inspecting it. His voice is low, modulated, private school educated.

A pleasant voice, Maggie concedes to herself. She grunts an agreement. The searing heat has settled in for January, testing tempers and keeping everyone busy.

The intruder tries again. 'What are you reading?'

Maggie lifts the cover, briefly.

'My mother adores Georgette Heyer.' Dr Elliott's golden-boy smile suggests he's fondly recalling his mother.

'Hmm.' Maggie keeps reading.

'Maggie,' he says, abruptly.

She looks at him, wary. 'Yes?'

The smile widens, grows intimate. Maggie's cheeks heat, despite herself.

'I was thinking how we got off to a bad start, ages ago, and we've never had a chance to be better acquainted.'

Maggie catches a scent of spicy aftershave, a fragrance she doesn't recognise. It discreetly murmurs 'expensive'.

He tilts his head, eyeing her left hand. 'You're no longer spoken for. Right?' His question is couched in a tease.

'Spoken for?' Maggie gathers the little energy she has. She closes the book and stands. 'If you mean am I no longer engaged, you're right. Not that it's any of your business.' She pushes in her chair, reaches up to check her cap and picks up the book. 'Nice to chat,' she says. 'See you around.'

'Bye, see you soon.' His voice is filled with amusement.

Later, after a meal with her parents of lamb chops, mashed potatoes and peas which she helped her mother shell, Maggie rings June and tells her about Dr Elliott's new charm attack. 'Am I going to be a target for every self-imagined heart-throb doctor?' she complains.

'Well, you're pretty, lively and intelligent.' June says. 'I can see you as a doctor's wife.' She pauses. 'Of course, you can get that ring back. If you want to.'

'Please, June. No more. And I don't want to be a doctor's wife. At least, not that doctor. Let's talk about your day, hey?'

Which is what they do, and Maggie forgets her misery for a good ten minutes. She hangs up, puts a shilling in the money box to help pay the bill, and decides it's time for bed. Early shift tomorrow.

Hauling herself from the telephone seat, Maggie walks from the living room into the hall, glancing into the kitchen where her mother is reading a magazine at the table. Nancy's wearing a loose, sleeveless dress in acknowledgement of the stuffy warmth of the room. Cigarette smoke swirls about her dark, permed hair like a winter storm. A mug of tea steams by her arm.

'Maggie,' she calls.

'Yes, Mum?' Maggie peers into the haze.

'Couldn't help overhear, something about a doctor?'

'Forget it, Mum.' Maggie rolls her eyes. 'Some silly peacock trying it on. Doctors are all the same, think every nurse is desperately in love with them.'

'Hmm.' Nancy stubs out the cigarette in a brimming glass ashtray. 'I have to say, love, it could be a good thing, this breakup with Arthur.'

Pain stabs at Maggie's heart at her mother's casual tone, the same she would use if Maggie decided to return a dress she didn't like. She waits in the doorway, guessing what the next sentence will be.

'I mean,' Nancy goes on, 'breakups hurt. Think about it, though. If Arthur was truly serious, you'd be well married with a couple of kids.' She squints at her daughter, who remains silent. 'You could do better, Mags, much better.'

'Thanks, Mum.' Maggie doesn't need to hide her ironic tone. Nancy has no notion of the concept, bless her. 'I'll bear that in mind.' She half turns. 'Off to bed, have a good night, see you tomorrow.'

'Sleep well, love.'

Maggie nods. She's weary after her long day. Hopefully tired enough to sleep well.

Chapter Four

LIBBY STRETCHES THE TELEPHONE CORD to its short, full length in an attempt to grab the cup of tea she dumped on the hospital staff room table when told the call was for her, sounded urgent. The twisted cord's not long enough, and there's no one else in the room to help her. She returns her attention to her brother, ranting at the other end of the line. Rob surprises her with his passion. So far, he has barely raised an eyebrow during the whole awful business of selling the family's cattle and sheep station to the Snowy Mountains Authority. Sailed through like it was happening to someone else.

'It's not my future Dad's giving up on,' he said to Libby when the Authority's decision to move the great dam first blew up. 'I never wanted to stay at grazing, don't much like cows, and despise sheep.'

It had been a Sunday, and Rob had driven Libby over from Cooma for the weekly family visit. One with a surprise attached to it when their father announced the battle with the Authority was over. The graziers had lost their legal fight. Nothing was left except to negotiate the highest prices for the land.

'Me and yer Mum are ready to retire, anyhow.' Dad scratched his sun-freckled bald head and squinted at his children as if seeing them for the first time. 'You both have yer jobs and yer lives in Cooma. Reckon we'd have to sell eventually.'

They sat around the long kitchen table covered with a clean seersucker cloth for Sunday lunch. Outside, frost clung to fences and trees, and the window above the sink was opaque with steam. The great cast iron wood-burning range filled the room with heat and the tantalising scent of roasting beef.

Selling made sense, expressed the way Dad told it. Which didn't stop nostalgia for her fun and free-ranging

The Past can Wait

childhood filling Libby's chest with a tight sorrow. She wouldn't be able to pass those experiences on to her own children, should she have them. Rob grunted, said, 'We're here to help when you need us,' which had been his longest sentence on the matter.

Until this afternoon, on the telephone to Libby at the hospital.

'Those bastards at the Authority,' he fumes, 'slow as a wet week getting these bloody promised payments out to the graziers.'

'It's early days, isn't it?'

'Not the point, Libs.' His voice is rough, like he's spoiling for a fight. He won't get it from her. 'They promised early money to give people plenty of time to get organised. Now they're mucking about like there's all the blasted time in the world.'

'What's Dad done about it?'

'Nothing.' Exasperation flows through the mouthpiece like the waters will flow through this new dam. 'Laid back and she'll be right, mate. His usual attitude.'

'Mum?'

'Fussing, worried, talks about having to pack up, except until they have somewhere to move to, how big the new place is, she can't decide what to pack, what to load in the ute for the rubbish tip, what to give to charities … Oh, and what do *we* want to keep?' He sighs heavily enough for the huff to reach her.

'Ages before she has to worry about sorting stuff.' This is her mother's way of coping, being busy for busy's sake. It will be driving her father up the wall.

'Once they have the money in the bank, they can make real plans,' Rob says. He's calmed, a fraction. 'I've tried calling the Authority myself.' He snorts. 'Those pig-headed bureaucrats won't talk to me. I'm a mere, no-account son.'

Libby cuts off his growl with an idea which excites her, and possibly not for the right reasons. 'Might be able to help,' she says. 'I *might* have an insider there.'

'Who?'

'Wait and see if it works, then I'll tell you.'

Libby promises to act immediately and hangs up.

Despite her promise, she doesn't reach straightaway for the telephone directory. Her pulse patters at the idea of an excuse to ring Arthur, her insider. He's popped in and out of her thoughts over the last two weeks, his warm voice murmuring his troubles, his brown eyes desperate for understanding, for sympathy. Libby absently collects her tea, takes a sip and spits the tepid liquid into the cup.

A cool voice reminds her that seeking out the company of broken-hearted men can never end well. Like when she tangled herself in knots over Alf, less than a year ago. She liked Alf a great deal, yet at the end of the day she'd been kidding herself, building castles in the air from the sand of polite conversation with a man already torn between two women.

Not a good idea to go there a second time, Libby, she chastises herself. Think of the state Arthur was in when you saw him. Why throw yourself under another bus of disappointment?

She deliberately sends her mind back to the conversation that warm night. A dispassionate analysis will banish her silly, schoolgirl flutterings.

The friend she'd had a post-shift drink with had left to see to husband and children. Libby was leaving too, her mind occupied with the exciting question of whether to have eggs on toast for dinner or open a tin of tomato soup. Her attention was caught by the tall, broad-shouldered man with the short brown beard who pushed open the hotel door. He lugged a suitcase, and his rumpled hair and creased clothes suggested he hadn't travelled first class. She didn't recognise him immediately. When the penny dropped, she called out instinctively, before it dawned on her – this close mate of Alf's was likely party to the full story of her humiliation at that man's hands.

Too late. Besides, she wanted company.

After re-introductions and a brief explanation of why Arthur was in Cooma, Libby suggested they head for the Italian café on Sharpe St, the town's main road, to share a bite to eat. Arthur's tiredness from two days of travel meant the conversation fell into silent dips which Libby bravely fought to scramble out from. Desperate, she peered at her companion around the lit candle in its wax-coated wine bottle and asked the question she didn't want to hear the answer to.

'How's June?' Carefully omitting mention of Alf. 'Must admit to being terrible at writing, lost touch a bit.'

Arthur laid his knife on top of his lasagna. 'Good. Settled in like she was born there, become great friends with … other nurses at the Royal, where she's working.' He took up the knife, cut into the pasta with the precision of a surgeon, releasing more of the aromatic deep red sauce and oozing bechamel.

Libby twirled her spaghetti around her fork, wishing she'd ordered a less difficult dish and wondering what the brief shadow was about, the one which had darkened Arthur's eyes when he talked about other nurses. Further news of June wasn't forthcoming, and the hesitation in Arthur's statement made her reluctant to ask. She tried a different tack.

'You're not up here forever, are you?' Libby dug a memory from the depths of her mind, something Alf said the first time she met Arthur. A girlfriend, another nurse, and the reason why Arthur was here. She dived in. 'Working on the Scheme to buy your girlfriend the house of her dreams, right? How's that going? Been a while.'

Libby's teasing smile melted when Arthur stopped eating. He stared at his plate. His jaw quivered. Libby's heart stopped. This big, rugged man was about to cry.

'Oh no,' she murmured. 'I've put my big foot in it like

always.' She reached across to place a hand on his arm. The bare skin with its mat of downy brown hairs was smooth and cool. 'I'm truly sorry, and understand if you don't want to talk about it, but I can be a good, sympathetic listener when I try.' She brought back the smile, gentle this time.

Arthur lifted his head, swallowed. 'You don't need to hear my troubles, Libby.'

'I might not need to. Seems to me, though, you could do with letting whatever it is out. It'll make you feel better, honest.'

'No,' he murmured.

'Yes,' Libby said. 'Think of me as, as–' she tapped the wax-encrusted wine bottle '–as that bottle, inanimate, not judging.'

The bottle tapping did the trick. It made Arthur smile, and it all came out. He told her yes, she was right, he was here saving for a house, and about Maggie's unwillingness to come to the mountains – her horror at the idea tamed down for Libby's native ears, she expects – and about the breakup.

Libby gazed into those gentle eyes, her hand on Arthur's solid arm, and understood in an intellectual way how great a change it would be for the woman. Yet she was not in the least on Maggie's side.

She's had no contact with Arthur since. Why should she? They're casual acquaintances, and Libby was a convenient shoulder to cry on. Maybe everything's sorted, the lovers re-united, the engagement renewed with fervour.

Dammit. Libby needs to get to the bottom of this, and there's only one way to find out. Besides, she rationalises, whatever her own motivations, she needs to do this for her parents' sake. Rob will kill her if she doesn't follow through on her rash promise.

She tosses the dregs of the cold tea into the sink, hauls the telephone directory onto the table and flips the pages to find the Authority's number in Adaminaby. It's not quite 5

The Past can Wait

pm, she might catch him. Taking a breath, she dials.

◇◇◇◇◇

Arthur has wasted pretty much a whole writing pad trying to write to Maggie. The crumpled, torn out pages fill the waste paper basket in his room at the boarding house. His landlady, Mrs Carter, empties the rubbish daily when Arthur is at work. Should she be curious to see what the scribbling is about and smooth the pages, she won't discover much. The longest missive Arthur has written has been two sentences along the lines of '~~Dear Maggie Dearest Maggie My darling Maggie~~ Dear Maggie, I am very very sorry and I miss you badly. Will you write to me please, tell me how you are feeling? I want to come home, to talk.'

Somehow, it doesn't seem enough despite the words being dragged from the depths of his soul. There's a Maggie-sized hole in his heart, a black space which devours all feeling.

At work, his hours are taken up with the moving of the town and its residents to the new site a few miles up the hill. Decisions need to be made, like which of the old public buildings are to be carefully taken apart, pieces numbered, loaded onto lorries and re-erected in their new locations like three-dimensional jigsaw puzzles. The church is one such building, an elegant yellow stone structure deserving to be saved. At the other extreme are the simple wooden frame houses which will be lifted from their foundations onto flatbed trucks and positioned in their spanking new bare gardens out of reach of the spreading waters.

Arthur has huge sympathy for the owners of those houses. They have paid for them, they are home with the memories, good and bad, they conjure. Neither the deep pockets of the Authority nor the threat of permanent flooding will break the emotional ties.

Then there are the preparations for the Guthega power station opening. He finds it impossible to enthuse like others on the team about the upcoming grand event.

After the day's work, he walks in the pale brown, low-lying hills surrounding the town, imagining when it will be under water. Adaminaby and thousands of acres of grazing land will form the bottom of the huge Eucumbene dam. A long history drowned, sunk out of sight for all time.

Arthur can't help pondering the parallels with his and Maggie's story, wincing inwardly at the melodrama. He sits on a boulder with the sinking sun behind him, the darkening shapes of cattle diminishing to dots on the far horizon. Is Maggie right? Is it time to let go of the old history driving him to pursue his dream?

The night – such a contrast to this empty, peaceful scene – is a scar on his brain. March 1943, and his family's Bethnal Green community reeled from the deaths of dozens of people in a stampede at an underground shelter. Among them were Arthur's grandparents, his father's parents, Judah and Esther Cohen. Arthur wasn't Arthur Kaine in those days. He was Aaron Cohen.

Arthur rises from the rock and walks along the rubbled dirt track towards the sparse lights of the town. His stomach grows nauseated remembering the whispered accusations of black marketeering by Jewish shop owners, of stones thrown by boys who had at one time at least tolerated him, occasionally called themselves friends. And the graffiti on the temporary fence shielding passersby from the worst of the horrors of bomb damage: 'Down with the filthy Jews.' How it came to a head when his people were blamed for the stampede, somehow, for some reason. No one ever bothered to explain. When exoneration was granted, it was too late.

Old history it might be. The spring evening his father came home – too early – from the grocery where he worked as an accounts clerk ... that history is as fresh as yesterday for Arthur.

He reaches the boarding house and lets himself in with his key. Mrs Carter's voice carries from the kitchen at the end of the hallway, together with the familiar smell of mutton stew.

'That you, Arthur?' His landlady walks out, wiping her hands on a tea-towel, her hair wrapped in its habitual scarf, her stockings wrinkling at the ankles below her plain brown frock. She nods at the telephone sitting on the table by the guests' sitting room door, the money box for users to pay for calls chained to the wall beside it.

'Call for you today, love.' She arches an eyebrow, briefly purses her lips. 'Not your sweet girl. Someone called Libby.' She points at the message pad. 'Got your number from the office. Left hers, wants you to ring her.'

Libby has called. Arthur reads the note on the message pad. *Libby Walters. Cooma hospital, Cooma 3222. Ring before 10 pm.*

Libby's on a shift, and Arthur has time to wonder why she would call him. Their conversation over the Italian meal the night he bumped into her has replayed in his mind in idle moments the last two weeks. His feelings seesaw from embarrassment at pouring out his heart to gratitude for being able to let out his grief to someone who wasn't involved. Libby offered no advice, neither did she assure him with cliches, such as things would turn out for the best. She listened, said how sorry she was, and wished him well. Arthur found it cathartic. On balance, his gratitude outweighs his embarrassment, especially as he decided he was unlikely to see her again.

Except, she's called, and manners demand he returns the call.

The hospital receptionist tells Arthur Libby will ring in her break. An hour later, she does.

'Hi, Arthur.' Her voice is bright, cheery. 'Sorry to bother you.' She coughs. 'I was wondering if I could ask a huge favour, and if you say I'm out of order, that's fine, except it's getting desperate and I'm hoping you can help.' Libby pauses, either to breathe or for him to respond.

Arthur is relieved the call doesn't have anything to do with his sad confessions.

'Umm, sure, if I can, whatever it's about,' he says. He has no clue what favour Libby could want until she tells him her father is one of the graziers the Authority is buying off.

'Ah,' he says, 'Right. To be honest, I haven't had much to do with those negotiations, been busy helping the townspeople sort themselves out.'

'It's not the negotiations,' Libby says. 'Done with. It's getting the actual pounds, shillings and pence in Dad's hands. It's taking far too long, and the family's worried.'

Arthur listens, murmurs his agreement that payments should be swift. 'Not sure what I can do,' he says. 'Those guys are pretty close-mouthed. All I can promise is to see what I can find out and get back to you.' He's not optimistic. The head of the team is a dour German, Karl Vogel. Rumour says Mr Vogel was a wealthy banker, pre-war. His team is tight, keep to themselves. Arthur suspects they're afraid of the tall, blond German with his deep blue piercing eyes and set mouth.

A grateful Libby gives him the telephone number of her flat. 'And Arthur,' she says as he's about to hang up, 'why don't you come out to the property for a visit one day?'

He frowns at the mouthpiece. 'A visit? I don't really think your parents would want to see me, an employee of the place forcing them to sell their livelihood.'

Libby's glee crackles down the poor line. 'You've got it wrong. Dad was about to retire, and given my brother isn't interested in farming, they would've sold up anyway. This saves them the hassle of finding a buyer, and the price is good.'

'Oh.' Arthur's pleased someone is happy with the dramatic change of plan. He hasn't come across many joyful faces recently. 'Good, and yes, in that case I'd love to visit.'

'Be treated as the hero.' Libby giggles. 'Which will mean

more than scones for afternoon tea. Hang on a sec.' Her muffled voice suggests she has put her hand over the mouthpiece. 'Finishing up, Matron, coming.' And to Arthur, 'Gotta go. Thanks heaps. Bye.'

'Bye.' Arthur speaks into a dead phone.

He replaces the handset in its cradle, wondering at the tingle of excitement in his stomach. It's because he can, possibly, help out a friend. Libby's request has given him a purpose. His instinct is to dial another number, much further away, tell Maggie this tidbit of news, share his sense of being useful. The tingle dies, overcome by the sadness which has taken up permanent residence deep inside him. Arthur breathes out heavily and makes his way to the kitchen to boil the kettle for tea.

Chapter Five

THE HEAT OF JANUARY HAS faded into the past. Maggie decides she'll need a light jacket to wear over her sleeveless blue and red dress this mild March evening.

It's an easier decision to make than the one to finally accept Luke Elliott's frequent invitations to see a film or let him treat her to a casual dinner. Neither of these events is happening tonight. Maggie is off to see a play, the first in her life. There wasn't much opportunity to see plays in London's war-ravaged East End, and since coming to Australia … well, plays haven't been what Maggie's group of friends do. Films, yes.

She flicks through the clothes in her varnished wood wardrobe and removes a navy linen jacket with white piping from its hanger, leaving the matching skirt behind. She bought the suit for June and Alf's wedding last spring, and the jacket will go well with the frock. The suit would be too dressy.

Slipping on the jacket, Maggie gazes into the full-length mirror which forms the panel between the wardrobe doors. She's lost weight since the beginning of the year. The jacket hangs loosely. The dress, which she sewed last summer, could do with taking in. She runs her hands through her hair, wishes for the thousandth time for straight, more manageable locks, and sighs. Why is she bothering?

Damn June and her bulldozer ways.

The two of them had grabbed a hasty lunch in the hospital canteen. When Dr Elliott spotted them and carried his tray to their table, Maggie eyed his approach with suspicion. Would he invite himself to join them? The mouthed 'no' she threw June went unheeded. June's attention was on the doctor, faint amusement playing on her lips.

'Hello, ladies.' Dr Elliott kept his tray held high. 'Good to see you're both as beautiful as ever.' He flashed his winning smile on June before turning to Maggie. 'I've tickets for the

Rep doing *Pygmalion* at the Tiv on Saturday, Maggie. Glad I've caught you here, because I was hoping to tempt you.' This smile was less flirtatious, more genuine. His eyes held an anxious gleam, anticipating another refusal.

June delayed it. 'What a treat,' she enthused. 'I've heard it's good, Maggie. You'd be supporting our own local theatre company too.'

Maggie had only the vaguest notion what *Pygmalion* was and no idea what the Rep or the Tiv meant. She frowned at June. 'If I had a clue …'

Dr Elliott blushed. 'I'm sorry, talking shorthand here, bad of me,' he stammered.

The blush and the stammer decided Maggie. 'You can explain when we're on our way.' She had him on the back foot at last, and it felt good. 'I'd love to come, thank you.' She smiled at him for the first time.

'Great!' His surprise touched her, and Maggie's self-worth smugly fluffed its feathers. 'I'll need an address to pick you up,' he said.

Time agreed – a matinee because the doctor would have a shift to work, and luckily it coincided with Maggie's time off – and details exchanged, the young doctor carried his tray to an empty table across the busy canteen. His step was bouncier than when he'd approached them.

'What have I agreed to?' Regret had already taken hold. Maggie wasn't ready for this. It was too soon.

June laughed. 'You've agreed to see a delightful play – it's about a young Cockney girl, actually. Being a Cockney yourself, you should find it highly entertaining.'

'Really?'

June ignored Maggie's sarcastic tone. 'And you've agreed to be driven there, no buses, by a handsome, well-off doctor.' She reached across to touch Maggie's hand. 'It's been nearly three months, Mags.' She shrugged. 'Luke Elliott may not be the man of your dreams, but he's determined.'

'And now he's caught me.'

'It's one outing, hardly even a date.' June withdrew her hand and stacked their dishes into a neat pile to carry to the counter. 'Of course you still grieve for Arthur. Natural after all those years together.' She shook her head. 'If you're not going to listen to my earlier advice and write to him, you need to get on with your life, see other men. And our doctor is a rather pleasant start.'

A pleasant start. Having been briefed about *Pygmalion* by her more widely read father, learned the Rep was the nickname for the state's Repertory Company (acting), and the Tiv was the Tivoli Theatre in town, Maggie is prepared for the outing. Intellectually, at least. Emotionally?

At the chime of the front doorbell, she startles out of her reverie. He's five minutes early. She swoops up her handbag, slips her feet into her navy Mary Janes and dashes for the door.

Her mother is there long before her, introducing herself, grinning, tossing her head like a flirtatious sixteen-year-old, and gushingly inviting Luke to come in, do please come in while Mags gets herself sorted. Luke is a match for the charm attack and grins in return, expresses his thrill at meeting Nancy and he can see where Maggie gets her beauty from.

Maggie's visceral urge to run to the safety of her room is thwarted by Luke's cheery, 'Hello, there you are. Looking great, Maggie.'

'Thanks,' she says, pushing past Nancy. 'I'm ready, shall we go? Bye, Mum,' and she has her date out the door, onto the porch, and heading along the white gravelled path to the wrought-iron gate in two heartbeats.

◇◇◇◇◇

'How did the launch go?' June offers Arthur roast potatoes.

'Thanks, June.' Arthur piles the vegetables onto his plate. He's missed good home-cooking, his landlady being what you might call a handy cook and no more.

He's glad to be home, taking time off after the busyness

of the Guthega Scheme opening at the end of last month. Although it's strange not seeing Maggie. More than strange. Her shadowed presence haunts him everywhere he goes, like a missing limb.

Like when Alf and June first moved into their new home. Maggie dragged him down here the first chance she had, showing him the sparkling modern kitchen, telling him she wanted one just the same. It's the kind of kitchen he once dreamed of building under Maggie's guidance, with wood-laminate cupboards, clean white counter-tops and a subtly patterned linoleum floor.

The stone of regret which weighs in his gut reminds him how abruptly dreams can end. Like the lavender evening sky seen beyond the sheer curtains above the sink, heralds the true end of summer.

'The launch?' Alf repeats. Having worked for a time on the Scheme, Alf's interest is understandable. June too, being a Cooma girl.

Arthur waves his fork. 'Smooth as silk, thank God, after the gigantic fuss and the planning down to how many biscuits people might eat.' He takes the gravy jug Alf offers him and is liberal with its contents, after checking his hosts have their share. 'Guthega's nothing like it was when Teddy worked there. He wouldn't recognise it.'

The sprawling camp of tents and temporary log buildings is swept away, together with the motley crew of workers from across Europe who created the clean-lined, square concrete power station with its pair of huge water pipes, the first to operate as part of the Scheme.

'Suspect he has no desire to recognise it.' Alf snorts, grins, and cuts his lamb.

'He and Raine going okay?' Arthur says.

'Yeah.' Alf's grin widens. 'Teddy's a responsible husband and dad these days, working hard in the shop, turning out exquisite furniture. Helps Raine with the kids too. She and her sister, Faye – you remember Faye? – are raking it in with their temp secretarial business.' He lays his knife on his plate and taps the side of his nose. 'Smart, the two of them.'

'Good.' Arthur peers closely, briefly, at Alf, who's sharing an arch, amused look with June. Seems Alf's completely over his obsession with Raine, having held a candle for her – mistakenly imagining it a secret – for how many years? Meeting up with June in the mountains last year was the best thing to happen to Alf.

Arthur's heart skips at the mutual adoration he witnesses. He concentrates on the meal, forlorn at the memory of his and Maggie's shared gazes, turning his blood hot, wanting to take her in his arms … He chivvies the emotions into hiding, searching for news other than the launch.

'Seen a friend of yours recently, June,' he says.

'Oh?'

'Libby, your nursing mate.' He turns to Alf. 'You knew her too, right?'

There are a few seconds of uncomfortable silence during which Alf blushingly nods, chews his food, and stares at his plate. What's going on? Has Arthur put his foot in it somehow? Irritation scratches his brain at the complexities of life. Damned if he's going to upset things by prodding around in the past. If he wants to hear about it, and he doesn't, not really, he'll ask Teddy. Or more likely Raine.

It's June who answers, ignoring the question to Alf. 'I must write to her,' she says with a moue of self-chastisement. 'Too easy to fall out of touch.' She smiles at Arthur. 'How come you've seen her? How is she?'

'Bumped into her in Cooma.' Arthur shifts in his chair. He doesn't elaborate on the circumstances or the conversation. 'And then she called me, asked if I could help her out with a family matter.' He fiddles with his cutlery. 'Her dad's one of the graziers the Authority bought off to move the big dam, and the buyers aren't in a hurry to settle up.'

'Of course. Old family, big landowners. A shame.' June

pauses, lifts a forkful of food. 'Could you help?'

'Hope so.' After Libby's call, Arthur had a short conversation with Kurt Vogel, the head of the team, and was surprised to discover him concerned and helpful. Kurt explained the problem was higher up the chain and he was already pushing. Arthur reported this to Libby, said he'd keep an eye on it, and they'd agreed a day for him to visit the Walters' property over Easter.

June moves on from money to more important issues. 'Is Libby ... with anyone these days?'

Alf pokes among the peas as if he's going to choose the best to eat, one at a time. Arthur's curiosity is piqued, and not about peas. This is not the time, however.

'No,' he says. 'She's not said, anyway.'

'Libby's so full of life. Wicked sense of humour too.' June persists with the conversation in the face of Alf's discomfort. Her eyes sparkle, and Arthur decides she has her own brand of wickedness. Must be those mountains. Need a sense of humour to survive what they throw at you.

◇◇◇◇◇

Maggie hangs the jacket, reaches around to unzip the dress. The play runs through her mind. Initially, she'd found the pompous Henry Higgins hilarious, and sympathised with poor Eliza's struggles to get her Cockney vowels under control. However, as the drama progressed, Maggie's unease progressed alongside. She snuck quick glances at her companion.

Was he making fun of her and her origins, her glottal stops and Cockney slang? Was the fancy doctor getting his revenge for her refusals? She bristled. His behaviour, however, was impeccable. Attentive, polite, making sure she had a drink to her taste at the interval, sharing hospital gossip. Relaxed and pleasant.

On the journey to her house, Luke chatted brightly about the play, its comedy and romance, filling in for Maggie's short, non-committal responses. He parked, walked her to the door with a sincere thank you for coming, he would catch her at the hospital, and he'd very much like to see her again. He didn't press for an immediate answer.

Maggie narrowed her eyes at the departing long-bonneted Chrysler coupe's jaunty progression along the suburban street. See him again? Unlikely, Doctor Elliott. She has no desire to expose herself a second time.

The good clothes returned to their hangers, Maggie slips into trousers and a light jumper and steels herself for her mother's interrogation over a late meal.

She scowls. Dealing with Nancy's unsubtle questions and, worse, hearing her mother draw unflattering comparisons with Arthur, is more than she can cope with. Her thoughts fly to June. Surely her supposed friend understood what Maggie was letting herself in for? Maggie's simmering anger at her perceived humiliation is June's fault, and the woman needs to hear about it.

Maggie sneaks past the kitchen where Nancy waits with tea and cigarettes, and into the living room. She quietly shuts the door and heads for the telephone.

◇◇◇◇◇

The phone on the hall table jangles a shrill summons. Alf jumps from his chair, which teeters on two legs before thudding upright. 'I'll go.' He rushes from the kitchen like devils are after him.

June giggles. 'Poor Alf,' she stage whispers, leaning confidentially towards Arthur. 'Libby had a real thing for him when he was up there. Did you know?'

Arthur didn't. It explains why Libby asked after June and not Alf. It explains Alf's shiftiness. 'Ah,' he says. 'Unrequited love.'

Alf re-appears. 'For you,' he tells June.
'Who is it?'

The innocent question sends Alf into a clown-faced pantomime. 'Um, er ... one of your nurse friends,' he blurts.

June's lips twitch. 'You mean Maggie.' She pushes from

the table and walks into the hall.

Alf slumps into his chair and regards Arthur with exhausted eyes. 'How are you doing, truthfully, mate? Any chance the two of you will get back together?'

Arthur slides his empty plate to the side. 'Maggie doesn't write. I haven't called.' He folds his arms on the table. 'Nothing in three months.'

'You want to get back?'

'Of course.' Loss squeezes the lungs in Arthur's chest. 'It wasn't my idea, this breakup.'

'Then a word to the wise.' Alf glances to the hall, from where the occasional murmured response to what must be a one-sided conversation wafts in the air. 'There's a doctor, at the Royal. Handsome, rich, and dead keen on our Maggie.' He says it softly, with such gentle tenderness that for a moment Arthur doesn't take it in.

'A doctor?' Arthur frowns. His loss grips harder, cutting his heart into a thousand ribbons. 'Maggie's seeing him?'

'First date this evening. Guess that's what the call's about, reporting in.' He relents. 'From what June tells me, Maggie wasn't too keen on going.'

'But she did.' Arthur's body is chill with despair.

Chapter Six

LEGS CURLED UNDER HER ON the sofa, Libby re-reads June's letter with true pleasure. It's been too long. She's missed her steady, quiet friend, despite June stealing Alf. Libby grins at the memory of her red-eyed, distraught self striding into June's flat that morning to vent her bitterness at Alf politely breaking the news there was no future for the two of them.

'There's someone else,' she'd moaned to June, who offered hankies and tea, dried Libby's tears and jollied her out of the depths of despair. And the moment Libby was out the door, June threw herself on the next bus south to Melbourne, where she fell into Alf's arms.

Libby sighs, enjoying her melancholy. The rest, as they say, is history. She's forgiven June. After all, June at least held off until Alf made it clear he had no interest in Libby. These days she can be truly pleased for them both. Her pride has recovered, which was all that was really hurt, she admits. She returns to the long letter.

A half dozen photos fell out of the envelope when Libby slit the edge, pictures of June's new home. She holds them to the light from the window above the sofa and peers curiously at the L-shaped red brick building with its concrete drive and low front fence. The young garden boasts a fledgling lawn bordered with saplings and squat bushes.

I've insisted on vegetable beds, June writes. *Alf's not keen. He'd have it given over to painted green concrete if I let him. As it is, I suspect it will be me mowing our patch of grass and certainly me weeding the beds.*

Quiet suburbia suits June. Libby taps a photograph against her lips, imagining herself in a similar house, with her own vegetables and rose bushes. She could like the idea. Depends who was mowing the lawn.

June says it was Arthur's visit which prompted her to

write. Likely this is why an image of Arthur fills Libby's mind. His chestnut tinged hair is longer than he wears it now, and rumpled in the breeze. He's wearing old trousers and a tatty shirt over his muscled chest, and he's pushing a mower. Libby watches through a café-curtained kitchen window, filling a jug with homemade lemonade to refresh her hard-working husband.

She savours the sense of togetherness, of sharing a life with someone, which the vision brings.

This coming Sunday, Arthur will go with Libby to her parents' home. She has told them she's bringing a friend for lunch, the man from the Authority who helped out with speeding up the money side. Her mother didn't pry, saying her daughter's guests were always welcome. Libby is eager for them to like Arthur. As she would be about any friend she took home.

Laying the photograph with the others on the side table, Libby ambles into the tiny kitchen to make a mug of coffee. Her mind still on Arthur, she goes through the motions of lighting the gas underneath the kettle, taking the jar of Nescafe from its shelf, and spooning the dark granules into the mug. Waiting for the water to boil, Libby's fingers tap the laminate countertop as she stares at the blustery autumn day outside. Sunday is Easter Sunday, the first of April, which gives her mother an excuse for killing the fatted calf for Libby's guest. Although, being Easter, it will be fatted lamb.

Libby recalls her mother's caring sympathy after the 'thing' – it was hardly a relationship, except in Libby's mind – with Alf. Loyal motherly murmurs about whoever this fellow was he was the one who lost out, and time to rest in the unhurried routine of the farm had gone a long way to restoring Libby's zest for life and confidence. There's not been another man since. Arthur coming into her life at this point is propitious.

The kettle's whistle is a warning siren, prompting Libby to

recall the ominous cloud of Arthur's ex-fiancée. Propitious might be optimistic. Arthur didn't want this breakup. He made that clear the night they went to the Italian restaurant. Heartbreak shone through his stolidly told tale as clearly as a lighthouse's beam, and with the same effect – bringing into sharp relief the rocks littering the path to safe harbour. Three months have passed. Is three months long enough to mend a broken heart?

Defensive measures are called for. Libby pours her coffee and leaves the mug on the kitchen table while she rummages in a drawer in the cracked varnished dresser for a writing pad and her fountain pen. She will confess to June how attractive she finds Arthur, and, assuming June knows Maggie, ask her friend to tell her whether the romance is properly, actually, truly over. June owes her that much.

◇◇◇◇◇

The pub in Adaminaby is quiet for a Saturday night. Arthur knows many of the Authority staff who live in the town have returned home for the Easter weekend, or, along with the locals, taken a holiday. The bright lights of Sydney might have drawn them, mothlike, to dance among the crowds for a few days.

Some dozen men are scattered about the hotel bar, alone or in twos or threes. With its unpolished, undulating planked floor, battered, mismatched chairs and tables, and warmed by a huge fire on this cool evening, the room is welcoming enough.

Arthur has nowhere else he wishes to be. Normally he would go home for Easter, add a day or two of vacation time to make the trip worthwhile. He knows his mother is disappointed he hasn't made the effort this year, pleading work pressures. Partly true. The other part of the truth is that home doesn't have the same pull it used to. Since his visit earlier in the month, he's written once to his mother to tell her about Easter, and nothing since.

The telephone call from Maggie to June the evening

Arthur visited, and Alf's cautionary news about a handsome, well-off doctor being keen on Maggie, hardened the hurt in Arthur's stomach. How can he compete with rich and good-looking? He doesn't ring family or friends, because he has no wish to hear more. He's happy for her, he tells himself. Good luck to her. Maggie will have a wonderful life, more than Arthur can ever offer.

Bitter misery renders his good intentions futile.

After swallowing a long swig of beer, Arthur replaces the glass schooner on the damp towel lining the bar. He'd like to get drunk tonight, a rare occurrence. He won't though. Libby is collecting him mid-morning for the promised visit to her family's property. He grimaces. He's not in the mood for meeting new people. And a hangover would make the day much more of a trial. He should ring Libby, make his excuses–

'Arthur. You stay in town?' Kurt Vogel, the finance man, stands beside Arthur. He holds a £1 note in his hand.

'Seems like it.' Arthur tempers his curt reply with a friendly, 'You too?'

Kurt nods, and orders a beer from the bartender.

The man scowls at the German accent. 'Schooner or pint?' His tone suggests he's talking a secret language the foreigner won't understand.

Kurt points to Arthur's drink, playing along. 'Das one.' His accent thickens.

Smugly placated, the bartender pulls the beer efficiently enough, with the right amount of foaming head.

Kurt thanks him, offers his money, and turns to Arthur. 'Yes, me also.' He lifts his drink from the bar. 'You would like company? I have no one to see.'

Arthur's too polite to say he'd prefer his own company. Or he has a phone call to make. Besides, he figures the bartender's attitude has been enough for the German for one night. He salutes Kurt with his beer. 'Sure, take a pew.'

Kurt frowns briefly before perching on a stool. Arthur

reminds himself that while the man's English is good, idioms might be beyond him.

Both take long draughts of their drinks. Kurt wipes foam from his smooth upper lip. 'Your Australian beer – this Toohey's? – is not so bad once you are used to it.' His lips twitch at his backhanded compliment.

Arthur shrugs. 'It wets the whistle.' He pauses. 'Thanks for helping with the Walters' payment, appreciate it.'

It's Kurt's turn to shrug. 'I would have paid everyone sooner. The delay is further up the ... chain?'

'That'd be right. Bureaucracy rules.'

Kurt's laugh has a rusty edge to it. 'Let us not talk about work.' He faces Arthur properly. 'Tell me why are you here in Adaminaby tonight? Do you not have a family to spend this holiday with?'

'Not here.' Arthur finishes his beer, sets the empty on the counter and beckons the bartender. 'Line you up one?' he says to Kurt.

Kurt holds up a hand which is smooth and long-fingered. 'Tonight we drink better than beer.' He sculls the remainder of his drink and addresses the bartender. 'A bottle of schnapps, please, apple if you have it.'

The bartender briefly raises an eyebrow before exploring the bottles lined up behind him. He selects one filled with liquid sunshine and places it before Kurt. A rummage under the bar results in two small, flute-shaped glasses which the bartender sets beside the bottle.

'Not a popular drink around these parts.' His stare borders on the polite side of belligerence. 'Used to be, once. Good for warming the innards on a snowy night.' He curls his lip, twists the curl into the semblance of a smile. 'Guessing you'd know about that, where you come from.'

Arthur grows warm at the man's continued, unsubtle rudeness. He himself has no reason to be fond of the German race, yet he tries to separate the individual from the whole, and not to assume.

Kurt's expression is bland. 'I do.' He offers money, and when the bartender returns with change, Kurt leaves it untouched.

'Let us sit there,' he says to Arthur, gesturing to an empty table near the fire. He grins and his eyes light with mischief. 'Not far to fall from a chair, hey?'

Arthur snorts. The notion he was going to call Libby surfaces for an instant, and scuttles to a dark crevice in his mind. The evening is early. She's likely on a shift. He'll call later, when she'll be at home.

The sunshine liquid works miracles to mollify Arthur's ongoing misery as it slides down his throat. Three glasses in, he's enjoying Kurt's sardonic wit as they talk easily about the Scheme, the launch last month, the townspeople's reactions to moving their homes three miles up the hill. The bar fills, the noise around them grows with the chatter of a dozen languages, the air thickens with wood and cigarette smoke, tinged with the scents of sweaty men and beer.

Arthur, less than sober, excuses himself to make a quick visit to the toilet outside and gulp cold air. When he returns, his head clearer, Kurt is staring into the coals of the smouldering fire. He rouses himself with a quick apologetic grin and pours each of them another glass.

'It is hard,' Kurt says to the bottle, 'to be the enemy, ten years on.'

Arthur understands the German is referring to the bartender. He ventures a tiny sip of schnapps.

'They said,' Kurt goes on in his deep, steady voice, 'there are opportunities to rebuild lives here in this so-young country.' He flicks a half-smile at Arthur. 'Your family? Ten pound Poms?'

'Yes. We took the Aussie government's money and shipped ourselves here in '48. Soon as we could leave.'

'Ah. It took me longer. I must first finish something before I could come searching for this new life.'

'Finish something?' Arthur lifts his glass for another tiny

mouthful of the sweet spirit. He has a sense he might need its comfort.

'A different search. For what was past. To hope it also can be the future.' Kurt throws back more schnapps, sets down the glass with steady hands. The look he gives Arthur is open, clear. If he's drunk, he holds his liquor well. 'I tell you this which I have not told anyone here. Is it okay?'

'Yes.' Arthur's not sure it is okay. There is tragedy here. War is an effective, if costly, machine for creating tragedy.

'Before ... before the war ...' Kurt pushes away his glass and rests his arms on the table. He bends his head to gaze at a round, fuzzy-edged stain. 'I was a banker. This I think everyone knows.' He flicks his eyes at Arthur, who nods. 'I was sent into the army even so, like every man, leaving my wife and my kinder – children – in Berlin.'

Arthur's lungs expand with human sympathy. It is clear what is coming. There is no wife and kinder with Kurt in Australia. He wants to ask the German to not tell him any more, to not scar his waking and sleeping moments, which carry sufficient scars already. Kurt stares into the fire, denying Arthur's chance to never know.

'Our house, it was damaged. Standing in ruined garden. Russian soldiers camping there. They sleep in my children's beds. They sleep in my and wife's bed. They eat off our plates, their hands on our knives and forks.'

Arthur clears his throat. 'Did you find them?' His voice is gentle.

'Ja.' The sound is a breath.

The noises of the bar around them sink into a silence so deep Arthur could dive into it and let it cover his head, drown him in sadness. For Kurt and his family, for his own family, all the families ... it's too much, too big for one man. He breathes out. 'I'm sorry.'

'Yes.' Kurt peers at him with glistening eyes. 'You are a good man, Arthur. I thank you.' He stands, grips the top of his chair. 'You will excuse me, bitte.'

Arthur follows the former banker's steady wending between the tables to the door. When Kurt pushes it open, the night sky fills the space, the stars a wash of diamonds scattered on a velvet blackness. This country is vast enough to swallow a thousand, ten thousand, personal horrors and give the sufferer space to find another way.

Arthur pushes from the table, pulls on his jacket and walks outside. In the short distance to the boarding house, he thinks that, whatever else happened – the injustices, the blame, the hatred, the name-calling and beatings – his own family is alive. They have a future, as a family. A future denied to Kurt.

The thought sobers him as effectively as the cold air.

He resolves to ring his mother in the morning, before Libby picks him up. Seems he'll be visiting her parents property after all.

Chapter Seven

ARTHUR WAKES TO EASTER SUNDAY bells tolling from the stone church, the one which will be dismantled and moved to the new town. Morning sun shows white at the edges of the brown roller blind. He grunts, rolls over and peers at the bedside travel alarm. Eight o'clock. Plenty of time before Libby collects him.

With reluctance, Arthur hauls himself to a sitting position, testing for a schnapps-induced headache. A slight tightness bands his forehead, his eyes are a little heavy. Otherwise, he's fine. He pushes off the sheet and the quilted bedspread, swings his legs out and plants his bare feet on the colourful rug which, in winter, is the one warmish spot on the white-painted wooden floor.

There's no smell of bacon from the boarding house kitchen because Sunday is Mrs Carter's day off from cooking breakfast. Arthur pushes his arms into his dressing gown, his feet into slippers and hurries to the bathroom. A chilly breeze lifts the curtain at the open window. He closes the window, cheered by the view of blue sky and white clouds. A beauty of a day for a trip to a farm.

Showered, and breakfasted on toast and instant coffee, Arthur pulls on a woollen jumper, leaves the boarding house and walks through the town to fully clear his head. Snatches of his conversation with Kurt surface in his mind, bubbling and sinking like the pictures he's seen of hot mud pools in New Zealand. He'd like to visit those for real one day.

Kurt. Poor bastard, losing his wife, his children, and God knows who else. Like millions of others. Bloody war.

When he returns, he rings his mother. The three minute trunk call is long enough for him to wish them a happy holiday, Easter not being a celebration in the former Cohen household. He establishes they are well, he is well, and yes, his mother had a letter from Arthur's sister recently. She too is thriving, as are his nephews and nieces. He tells his mother he loves her, is thrilled at her delighted gasp, and the pips sound. Time is up.

Arthur sets down the receiver with a new lightness in his chest. They are well. They are thriving. There is a new generation growing up away from persecution and hatred, without tragic memories. The day ahead is no longer a burden. He will enjoy being with a family for a time, even if it's not his own.

At ten o'clock, Arthur's on the verandah, his best tweed coat over his arm. A bag containing an Easter egg for Libby and a gift of chocolates for her mother waits at his feet. Libby arrives five minutes later in an elderly, dusty, black Ford Prefect. Braking to a sudden halt, the car barely ceases to move before Libby's out the driver's door. She's wearing denim jeans, brown boots, a green and red flannel shirt and a deep green corduroy jacket. Her long auburn hair is tied in a ponytail.

'Morning,' Libby calls, bouncing up the two steps to the verandah.

Her energy lifts Arthur's mood higher.

She eyes the crisp crease in his trousers, moves her gaze slowly up to his white shirt and thin tie, takes in the coat over his arm. A mocking sigh is followed by a grin. 'I did say we're going to a farm, didn't I?'

'Umm, yeah, sure. I thought … Sunday lunch, Easter … I should make an effort? Be polite?'

Libby shifts her grin to a delighted smile. 'Sweet. Now. Should I make you change or let you impress Mum with your manners?'

'I'd rather impress your mum.' Arthur fingers the tie. 'This instrument of torture could go?'

'No.' Libby tips her head to the side and rapidly bats her eyelashes. 'We women love a man in a tie.' She shrugs. 'Leave it, you can take it off when I give you the tour and–' she peers at his lace-up work shoes '–we can find a pair of gumboots to fit you. Loads of them in the boot room.'

Wardrobe sorted, Arthur's idea about offering to drive is banished by Libby's confident stride to the car, where she tucks herself behind the steering wheel.

'Ready?' she says once Arthur, his coat and bag are settled in the passenger seat.

The interior smells of clean straw dust. Pale golden strands are scattered in the footwell and on the rear seat.

'It's not far.' Libby presses the clutch, turns the key, gives Arthur a thumbs up when the engine roars into life – this is a triumph of some sort – jerks the gear stick into first and manoeuvres the car to face the way she arrived.

Arthur wishes the journey could be longer. Recent rains have cast a lush green tint to the undulating landscape where sheep and cattle graze behind wooden stock fences. In the near distance, the greenery gives way to blue hills. They drive along a ridge on a stony dirt track, giving Arthur a view of range after range of mountains melding in the distance into the blue of the sky.

'Magnificent country,' he says.

'Yes. Shame it'll soon be under water.' Libby's tone is dispassionate.

Arthur's discomfort at representing those undertaking this massive transformation of the land is soon replaced with embarrassment by the warmth of his welcome at the homestead. Mrs Walters' effusive thanks for both the chocolates and for 'ripping through the Authority's bureaucracy like a dose of salts', heat his cheeks and cause him to stumble over his protests, he didn't do much, simply brought it to the attention of the right person, the finance man … which is brushed aside. He's more comfortable when Mr Walters teases him about his creased trousers and tie, earning the man a gentle slap from his wife.

'Leave him be, Tom.' Mrs Walters winks at Arthur. 'We women love a man in a tie. Goodness knows it's a rare sight round these paddocks.'

As Libby foretold, the meal is fit for a hero. Arthur

relishes each mouthful of tender lamb, each perfectly browned roast potato and homegrown peas and carrots. He hasn't eaten this well since his last trip home.

The conversation revolves around Mr and Mrs Walters' plans, given the Authority's money is in the bank.

'Get rid of this clutter to start with.' Libby's mother gestures at the over-furnished dining room.

Massive dressers filled with teetering piles of crockery shoved haphazardly among books and magazines are interspersed with paintings of English landscapes to fill the walls. The occasional portrait of a prize specimen of beef cattle or woolly sheep complements the sombre-hued hills and millstreams. Heavy drapes are pulled apart, with yellowing venetian blinds filtering the light. The carpet is spotless, including the bare patches.

'Get rid of the clutter, she says.' Mr Walters' affectionate eyes contradict his growl. 'Betcha half of it ends up in the new place.'

'I'll make sure it doesn't.' Libby waggles a chiding finger, her face lit with fun. 'New house, new beginnings.'

For sweets – over the years Arthur has learned this Australian term for what he calls pudding and the upper classes call dessert – there's rhubarb crumble with silky hot custard. After a second helping, Arthur sits back in the padded dining room chair, pats his stomach and compliments his hostess on the meal.

'Thank you, love,' Mrs Walters says. And to Libby. 'Don't worry about the washing up, Libs. Me and Dad'll sort it. You show Arthur around.' She gives her guest a sly look. 'Bet he'd enjoy a walk after two helpings of custard.'

The brown lace-ups are exchanged for tall, black gumboots a tad too large, the tie discarded, and Arthur decides the sun's warmth makes his tweed coat redundant. He follows Libby out of the enclosed verandah to follow a path past a patch of lawn, a cluster of fruit trees where apples hang ready for picking, vegetable beds cleared of their summer harvest and waiting for winter plantings, and through a crooked gate. Wood and corrugated iron outbuildings of different sizes form an uneven perimeter around a sparsely grassed square, the long shearing shed at the furthermost point. Mingled scents of hay, dust, old machinery and livestock carry on the warm air.

He and Libby perch on a tall wooden fence surrounding one of the many pens. The afternoon breeze plays lightly with Arthur's hair, the sun kisses his face. His ease verges on contentment.

'You'll miss this, won't you?' he says.

'Yes.' Libby pulls out her ponytail, redoes it. 'It's okay. Mum and Dad are happy and that's what counts.' She twists to face Arthur. 'Do you miss where you grew up?'

'Hardly. We didn't have anything like this.' He waves a hand to take in the paddocks, the house, the mountains. 'It wasn't too bad before the war.' He conjures the tiny terrace house where he, his parents and older sister, were content enough. His friends too, as they were then, playing football in the narrow streets, being shouted at by old Mrs Cooper when they accidentally hit her pot of geraniums on her windowsill. 'Then stuff happened.'

'The war.'

'Yes.'

It must be the catch in his voice which makes Libby ask, 'Not just the war?'

'No. All part of the same great mess though.' Arthur shifts his grip on the railing and gazes at the homestead. 'London wasn't a good place for people like us.'

'Like us?'

There's no reason to be secretive, not these days.

'I wasn't born Arthur Kaine.' He turns to Libby's questioning face. 'My given name is Aaron Cohen.'

Her eyes gleam with understanding. 'You were in England. Weren't you safe there?'

'Safe as in no one rounded us up into concentration

camps.' Arthur pauses. While the fear from those times has faded with the years, the memory of it remains real. The gasping hole in his chest, unable to breathe, all sense of safety, of security, of home, ripped from him. 'It wasn't exactly hunky dory,' he says at last, with dry humour.

Libby waits.

And he tells her what he has told no one except Maggie. About the hatred, about the shelter stampede and how it was blamed on the Jews, about his father losing his job, the endless search for new employment. About being forced from their home, the landlord deciding he needed it, after twelve years of the Cohens living there, for relatives made homeless by the bombing. The Jewish families were the ones thrown out of their houses.

'We spent the rest of the war living in one room. Dad finally landed a job with the Army, in logistics, based in London. There was money then. No houses. Not for us.'

Arthur hears himself tell the story in the same way he told it to Maggie. No, not in the same way. With Maggie, he'd been full of the passion of injustice, venting his anger, the unfairness of it. Maggie understood. She'd been there. Now, telling it to Libby, he is more matter-of-fact. This is what happened.

And, with Kurt's tale chiming in his head, a new gratitude, like the first, tender pink skin forming over a wound. *We've come through it, my family has come through it, alive and whole.*

'I can see why you emigrated,' Libby murmurs.

'Best decision the old man ever made, though not sure he needed to change our names. Makes him more secure even here ... I guess ...' Arthur laughs, breaking the solemnity. 'My sister didn't come with us. She married a GI and went to America. We could've gone to Canada, been closer to her. My mum refused. Sold on the sunshine she was, wanted to come here.' Arthur waves at the vast expanse of sky, at the white clouds building over the far ranges. 'This is what she came for, and the heat.'

'Wise of her not to come all the way up here.' Libby shivers, wraps her arms around herself. The afternoon has cooled, the breeze more lively. 'Might not have found the winters much to her liking.'

Arthur feels the lack of his coat. 'Winter can be pretty rugged, for sure.'

Libby jumps from the fence. 'Thanks for telling me,' she says. 'We can't begin to understand here what people suffered.' The strengthening wind whips her ponytail around and she pushes it over her shoulder. 'I mean, a lot of local families lost husbands and sons in the war, which was dreadful. The rest of us–' She pauses. 'We went on with our lives, our biggest complaint being about a bit of petrol rationing.'

Arthur lowers himself to the packed earth. The short telling of his story has left him weary and embarrassed. What is it about this woman which makes him open up to her? One-sided too. He knows nothing about her own life outside of her parents and this property. What of her own heartbreaks, her own wants and needs? He squirms, remembering June's comment about Libby and Alf. He pushes the thought away. Irrelevant.

'We got lucky,' he says. 'It worked out for us in the end.' He recalls Kurt's breathed, 'Ja,' in answer to Arthur's question last night, whether he found his wife and children. A new perspective on terrible. 'A lot worse happened.'

'Yes, it did. A lot worse.' Libby lightly smacks the wooden fence. 'While I could stay and talk forever, we have to be heading off.' She sighs dramatically. 'Early shift in the morning and I need my beauty sleep.'

They walk to the house where Arthur is as effusive in his thanks to the Walters as Libby's mother was to him. He is told it was a pleasure to have him, he must come another time, and Libby will make sure he does, right, Libby? Libby nods with enthusiasm and hugs her parents farewell.

The Past can Wait

The short journey is made in comfortable silence. When they arrive at the boarding house, Arthur questions Libby about driving in the dark to Cooma on the rough roads. Laughing, she tells him not to fuss, she's done it a thousand times in worse than darkness.

She gets out of the car to say goodbye, standing close to Arthur. She's tall, their eyes nearly on a level, hers gleaming green in the light from the porch.

'Thanks for showing me the farm,' Arthur says.

'It was fun.' The gleam becomes mischievous. 'I think Mum's decided to adopt you – two helpings of rhubarb crumble *and* hurrying up the money …' Libby stretches on her toes, and lightly kisses Arthur's cheek. 'I'll see you soon,' she says, walks swiftly to the car and revs the engine.

Arthur follows the tail lights down the hill out of the town. It *was* fun. His thoughts turn to Maggie. She'd love the Walters. If she was willing, he should drag her up here, show her what kind of people inhabit this remote country. If … The ache in his chest re-awakens, stretches its metaphorical arms to push at his rib cage. Maggie's feelings about the mountains are clear. Arthur can grudgingly understand. She didn't have an easy war, either, and being uprooted once more … He shouldn't have asked, he should have understood her well enough to not be caught off-guard by her outburst.

After nearly six years, the mountains have gotten under Arthur's skin. When he goes home, the noise, the people, the lights, the rush, push him into himself. He wants to curl up in a ball – with Maggie tucked into his body – and forget the hurried world exists. He exhales heavily. And him a Londoner! Maybe that's why. It's the contrast.

The night air is cold. Arthur stirs himself from his spot on the verandah, pulls his key from his jacket pocket and lets himself into the house. A radio blares from the kitchen at the end of the hall. Yellow light pools on the floor under the closed door. There's warmth and welcome here. But it's not home, never could be. This is not where he wants to be in a year, two years' time, living in a boarding house.

Arthur reaches his room and plumps onto the bed. His hand goes to his cheek, to the spot where Libby kissed him. She's a lovely woman, bubbly, sympathetic. An image of her lustrous ponytail whipped by the wind as they sat on the fence, makes him smile. Attractive too. It amazes him she isn't married, doesn't have a boyfriend. She can't be mooning over Alf still? Likely there's been another boyfriend since. He should ask some time. He'd like to know her better.

Shrugging out of his jacket, Arthur replaces it with his jumper and digs around in the chest of drawers. He pulls out his pen and, from behind the used-up writing pad, the blue airmail envelope he bought last time he was in Cooma. He'll finally write his long overdue letter to his sister in Canada.

⋄⋄⋄⋄⋄

Libby should be in bed, getting the beauty sleep she said she needed. Useless to try. Saying goodbye to Arthur at the boarding house doesn't mean her brain, and emotions, have finished with him for the day.

Wrapped in a blanket over her pyjamas, her hair in a nighttime plait, Libby stretches her legs, knees bent, across the two seats of her sofa and cradles a mug of cocoa. The room is lit by a standard lamp, cosily shadowed. Exactly the right atmosphere for thinking, which is what she is doing. Hard thinking.

The day replays in her head like a record on a turntable, except instead of lifting the needle and changing the record at the place where she kissed Arthur's cheek, Libby re-sets it at the beginning. She sees the approving gleam in her mother's eye when Arthur presented her with his gift of chocolates, and how her approval grew at his appreciation of the meal and his attentiveness to her father's long explanations about the workings of the property.

What's engraved on her mind – no, on her soul – is

The Past can Wait

her and Arthur's conversation at the stock fence. He, and millions of others, went through all variations of hell during the war. Arthur deserves a bright future, like Libby has enjoyed a happy past. She is grateful, for the farm, her family, her nursing. It would be good, she decides, to share her good fortune, help another person be content as she should be content.

Libby sips the hot cocoa and lets her heart tell her there's no doubt she finds Arthur attractive. This Maggie is a madwoman to pass up the chance of marrying him. He's sensitive, caring, good looking.

Maggie. Libby has avoided the question of Maggie all day, including on her solo drive to Cooma, and this evening. She knows she can't do so forever. What is she like, this woman? Does she miss Arthur, wants him by her side, to marry him as she promised?

Setting the cocoa on the side table, Libby unwraps herself from the blanket and pads in her socks to the dresser. The drawer sticks when she tugs it, and she grunts with annoyance. It opens sufficiently for her to reach in and pull out the writing pad which contains the unfinished letter to June. Libby forages for her fountain pen, an envelope and a stamp, and carries her collection to the kitchen table. With the blanket over her shoulders, she runs her eye over the half page she wrote when she first received June's letter. A hello, thanks for getting in touch, love the pictures. She taps the pen against her cheek and begins to scrawl.

I'm guessing you must know Maggie, Arthur's ex-fiancée, she writes. And stares into space. Best to be blunt. *Arthur came out to the farm today. He's been helping Mum and Dad with some Authority business, sorted now. There's only one way to say this, June, and I want you to be honest with me because I can't go through THAT again. You know what I mean. Is it honestly over between them? With love, Libby.*

June will imply the rest. Libby needn't spell it out. Before she can change her mind, she throws her long winter coat over her pyjamas, pulls on her boots and leaves the flat. There's a post box at the end of the street. Libby holds the letter at the slot, pulls it back, whispers, 'Nothing ventured' … and slides her naked plea into the unforgiving darkness.

Chapter Eight

MAGGIE TOYS WITH HER TOASTED sandwich and stares past June through the window of the café. Heavy rain blurs the scene of pedestrians hurrying along the footpath with umbrellas close to their bent heads. A woman in a red raincoat loses the battle with the blustery autumn wind. Her umbrella tears itself inside out, tugging at the woman's hand in a reckless bid for freedom. She scurries on, out of Maggie's view.

'Do you think he's making fun of me?' Maggie shifts her gaze to June, sitting opposite, spooning up chicken soup.

June frowns, pauses her meal to continue the conversation about the motives, perceived or otherwise, of Dr Elliott's pursuit of Maggie. 'No, I don't.' She waves her spoon. 'Can't you see how patient he's been with your constant dithering, not giving the poor man a straight answer when he asks you out?'

'Hmm.' Maggie acknowledges the truth of this. Since the play, she has been cowardly enough to offer ever less valid excuses to refuse Luke's frequent invitations. She should tell him outright she's not interested. June, however, urges her to accept, to take a chance. She lifts a square of sandwich and bites into it. The hot melted cheese tingles on her tongue.

'Hmm what?'

Maggie swallows. She takes in the other customers, all women in this frilly, over-decorated pretending-to-be-Parisian café. Many wear hats, gloves on the table beside their plates, shopping bags at their feet. Others are dressed in pencil skirts and tailored jackets. Secretaries, Maggie guesses. Everyone is deep in their own bits of gossip.

'Why would someone like him be interested in me?' she challenges. 'Do you know where he was over Easter?'

'No, where?'

'Visiting his grandparents across the border. I guess they

own half the state, a huge property in the Western District.' Maggie scowls. 'They're *rich*, an old family.' She snorts. 'No doubt they played polo and had the butler serve tea on the lawn.'

'And?'

Maggie wipes her fingers on the rose-coloured serviette and scrunches it into a ball. 'And what on earth would a man like him want with *me*, a Pommie immigrant from the East End?'

June won't be budged. 'This is Australia,' she says, 'not your class-ridden England. Perhaps he's in love with you.'

Folded arms across her chest, Maggie grins. 'You're such an optimist, June. I love you for that.'

June returns the grin. 'Usually you're the optimist.' Elbow on table, she lifts her hand, palm up. 'The real question is, do you like Dr Elliott? Do you, underneath this nonsense about making fun of you, want to keep seeing him?'

Maggie considers the question. She thinks about how Luke's confident eyes gaze on the world, his restrained smile suggesting all life amuses him. How the way he runs his hands through his curls sets the pulse thudding of every woman within a mile.

He's been the one to seek her out, as dogged as a terrier after a rat. There are plenty of other, prettier nurses who would jump at the chance to be seen on Dr Elliott's arm. He's polite to these eyelid-batting girls, and will banter with them on ward rounds, entertaining patients like Mrs Harrington. Nobody could take his behaviour to mean more than fun.

'Ha!' Maggie's mood lifts. 'If it's only to watch the other nurses' eyes turn green with jealousy, then yes.'

Their giggles attract disapproving glares.

'And ...' June hesitates, neatly folds her serviette. 'And ... Arthur?'

Maggie's pulse jumps at the question. 'What about him?' Her question is sharper than it should be, defensive at what sounds like an accusation of infidelity.

June frowns. 'I mean, are you and Arthur really over?'

Really over. Maggie rolls the words silently on her tongue, tasting the bitterness. Four months, and Arthur hasn't written or rung her. Neither has she written or called him. She glances to the ceiling. Arthur's image plays in her mind, his distress at the party, his voice calling after her, how she ignored him, eaten up by her own disappointment and anger. Hurt swamps her, together with the sense of loss, the hole in her life which refuses to close. Could Luke Elliott close that hole?

'We have to be over, don't we? I can't wait around for him forever.'

Her brusque response is met with June's sympathetic touch to her arm. 'No, you can't. And as I've tried to say a thousand times, getting on with your life is what's important.'

Maggie presses her lips into a mocking smile. 'And as you've also said at least a hundred times, our doctor is a good place to start.' Her hurt is soothed by this commonsense approach. At least for now.

June wags her finger. 'This is true. Meanwhile …' She blushes pale pink. 'Moving on from you to me, I've some news.'

It takes Maggie two heartbeats. 'You're going to have a baby?' Her shout is heard by everyone in the room.

June nods, beetroot-faced and grinning like a clown at the fun fair. Maggie jumps from her seat to grab her friend in a tight hug, uncaring of the amused, congratulatory smiles of other customers. The news stirs a flurry of emotions which crowd the space where the soothed hurt lives. She's thrilled, of course she is. Her happiness for June, and for Alf, overflows into bursts of giggles.

Yet, deep in the place she keeps her most secret feelings, a shard of envy stabs at her happiness, as green as the nurses' jealous eyes. Maggie's chances of holding her own baby in her arms are receding by the day.

'My birthday,' Luke tells Maggie, 'and everyone insists on a party.' He does the thing running his hand through his hair and adds a self-effacing moue.

They are walking to his car after watching *A Town Like Alice* at the Metro in Hindley Street. Luke is about to go on shift and must return to the hospital. Maggie will walk with him as far as the bus stop and make her way home from there. The clear May night is mild, the stars a pale silver wash above the city's glow.

This is their third outing, after the play and a visit to the Art Gallery, not far from the hospital. Luke took her there on an impulse, coaxing her from her canteen lunch by pointing out the sun shone and a short walk would be good for them both.

Maggie was about to shake her head, say no thank you, I should already be in the wards.

'Please?' Luke said, softly.

June's exhortations to give the man a chance played in Maggie's head. 'Okay,' she said, unsmiling. A walk in the sunshine was harmless, could hardly be called a date.

She was gratified by Luke's surprised delight. More so by the glimpse of two narrow-eyed nurses following her and the doctor's progress from the canteen, his hand steering her, in gentlemanly fashion, between the tables. She held her head higher and her grin in.

Passing the Gallery, he pulled her inside, saying he wanted to show her something, a favourite piece of his since he was a kid. Maggie allowed herself to be drawn by his enthusiasm.

Luke led her to stand before a delicate, pastel water colour of sparsely wooded scrub fronting an isolated craggy outcrop.

'It's by Albert Namatjira, the aboriginal artist,' he said. 'The Gallery bought it long ago, in 1939.' He folded his arms to examine the painting. 'The way it captures the colours of the outback are so true to life, don't you think?'

Maggie confessed she'd never seen the outback, and Luke had said, 'One day you will,' like a promise.

Maggie likes the way Luke treats her. On this film outing, he complimented her clothes, her hair, guided her to her seat and made sure she was comfortable before sitting himself. At the interval he bought choc-coated ice cream cones from a harassed vendor with her wooden tray slung about her neck. Maggie was amused at the natural way he dealt with the transaction, making the girl giggle.

She feels good when she's with Luke. Thoughts of Eliza Doolittle have been banished, and she can be amused by her suspicions. Probably, like June, he considered Maggie would find it hilarious. Damned Australians and their warped senses of what's funny.

Walking along the road, Maggie is yet to allow the jangle of tram bells and the low growl of cars to drag her from the film's gratifying lovers' reunion in the heart of Australia. She marvels at human resilience and wonders if, had it been a true story, the heroine would have gone on to settle in the outback town, persuaded by her love for her soldier. Hmm. Maggie squirms. The film is suddenly less gratifying. Anyway, she justifies, the heroine's wretched experiences of the Malayan jungle are a lot different from Maggie's comfortable daily existence. There's no comparison.

'You'll come?'

Luke's question jolts Maggie back to the present.

'Come where?' she says. 'Sorry, I was off with the fairies.'

'My birthday party, Saturday.'

'This coming Saturday? Three days' time?'

More hand running through the hair. 'Sorry for the short notice, Maggie. To be honest, I wasn't sure you'd want to come. I hope you do though. It'll be fun, lots of friends there, music, food.' Luke laughs. 'Party stuff.'

'I have to work.' Maggie sits on the fence of regret. She loves a party and hasn't been to one since the New Year disaster. On the other hand, what on earth has she to wear to what will surely be a posh frock do?

'Someone will swap shifts with you,' Luke says. 'What about your lovely friend? What's her name? Jane, Julie?'

'June. And I'm not sure I want to ask her.' Because June is having a baby and needs rest when she can get it. Maggie doesn't say this to Luke.

'Another nurse must need a favour, swapping out another Saturday.'

He appears keen for her to come, despite the late invite. Was he genuine when he said he worried she'd say no? Or is it because Maggie, even dressed to the nines and educated about Albert Namatjira, won't fit in with his crowd? She squashes the possible insult. A party is a party, and she needs cheering up.

They reach the bus stop. Luke waits for an answer.

'I'll try my best and get back to you,' Maggie says.

He kisses her lightly on the cheek, takes her hand in his soft, warm one. 'Try hard. I'd love you to meet my friends.' He strides up the Terrace to the hospital, checking his watch as he goes.

The bus is empty bar a man in a brown suit reading yesterday's newspaper and a young couple cuddling at the rear. Maggie takes a seat at the front and rests her head on the cool glass. June is right. She needs to get on with the rest of her life. Now she's taken these first steps with Luke, a party doesn't seem too difficult. It will be fun.

She closes her eyes and decides to accept the invite if a shift replacement can be found. Having made the important decision, Maggie's mind picks over the contents of her wardrobe. It's a waste of thinking time. The old cupboard holds nothing in the way of formal dresses.

At home, she rings June.

'Birthday party? Nothing to wear?' June says at the end of Maggie's garbled plea for help.

'Saturday, this Saturday. And I have day shifts, no

chance to go shopping supposing I could afford anything worthwhile.' Maggie sighs into the mouthpiece. Life with Arthur was never this complicated. 'I should say no, can't find anyone to swap–'

'Enid was asking the other day,' June says. 'Her sister's wedding is the following Saturday. She was begging people. No one was interested.'

'We might be if she ever went out of her way to help the rest of us.' Enid's reputation for putting what's best for Enid first, last and in the middle is well known. 'Sounds like that part of the problem is sorted, then.' Maggie humphs. 'There's still the dress.'

'Hmm, might be able to help out. I've something I've worn a grand sum of twice.'

Maggie barks a laugh. 'I've lost weight, sure. I still couldn't fit into something of yours, Mrs Skinny.'

Maggie has had to move buttons on trousers and skirts to tighten them around her waist. Not enough, however, to squeeze her hips into a frock June's size. Thanking her friend, Maggie hangs up. She twists on the telephone stool to stand, and startles. Her mother is there. For once, Nancy doesn't have a cigarette in her hand.

'What's the dress for?' Nancy's eyebrows arch.

When Maggie tells about the invite, her mother's eyes light with satisfaction. 'Introducing you to his family and friends. Good sign, Mags, good sign.'

'Family?' Luke didn't mention family.

'Well of course his family'll be there. At their house, isn't it?'

'Well, yes …' Maggie's reluctance about the whole plan resurfaces. Is she going to be introduced to Luke's family as his girlfriend? Is she his girlfriend? She thinks of the kiss on the cheek. A friendly kiss, no passion in it. Not like Arthur's long, warm kisses. Maggie could melt into those like a swooning heroine, even after five years. She shakes herself out of remembering.

'Mum.' She adopts her firmest no-nonsense voice. 'Dr Elliott is a friend, that's it.'

Nancy reaches into her cardigan pocket for her cigarettes, draws one out and puts it in her mouth while patting her clothes for a lighter. 'Not for much longer, my girl,' she mumbles around the cigarette. 'I'll go shopping tomorrow. Trust your old mum to find the perfect set of glad rags for this knees-up. You'll be the belle of the ball.'

Nancy's taste in clothes runs to the garish at worst, the colourful at best. Maggie wrinkles her nose. 'Buy it from somewhere you can return it, Mum,' she mutters, and works out how to tell Luke she can't make it.

Chapter Nine

LIBBY HAS GIVEN UP HOPING for a response to her letter to June. Maybe her own missive is lost in the post. It did have a long way to go. Or June's silence is a strong hint Libby should back off, matters aren't resolved between Maggie and Arthur one way or the other, her new friend needs more time. If this is the case, Libby is put out that her feelings are secondary. June could at least tell her Arthur is off limits, not freeze her out like this.

As she goes about her workday, changing beds, giving out medication, showing new mothers how to bathe their writhing newborns, fragments of memory of Arthur sitting next to her on the fence confiding his broken past dip in and out of her mind. She's tempted to ring him despite not knowing where things stand. No, she won't do that. Libby has learned from the past.

The post finally rewards her for her patience. Returning home one cool evening, she finds a letter with June's handwriting on the creamy envelope. Libby doesn't open it immediately. Placing the letter on the kitchen table, she moves to the bedroom to change out of her uniform and into warm trousers and a bulky jumper. The flat is chilly, and she switches on the electric radiator.

Libby's flat is one of four in a converted old house, and she is lucky enough to have claimed the former family living room with its Victorian fireplace and cast iron grate. She eyes the wicker basket of kindling and small logs sitting on the tiled hearth. If the news is good, she'll light a fire and dig out the bottle of Mateus Rose she's been saving for a special occasion.

Still she doesn't open the letter. Working around the envelope with the same care she would work around a wild horse needing to be tamed, Libby prepares herself an evening meal of eggs on toast and a pot of tea. She eats the eggs slowly, dainty bites, stretching out the time until the last mouthfuls are of cold yolk and soggy bread.

The tea remains warm under the pink and green striped tea cosy Libby knitted when she was twelve years old. She pours out a cup, carries it to the table by the sofa and returns to the kitchen for the envelope. Placing the letter by the cup, she goes to the dresser, jerks open the stuck drawer and delves for an opener.

A sip of tea, and Libby finally cracks. Dragging her gaze from the dull bars of the radiator, she curls her legs under her with appropriate resolution and slits open the letter. Not one of June's long missives, no photographs. A single page of the copperplate handwriting.

Libby scans the words. By the end, she is smiling.

June apologises, has put off writing until she could say something definite. The right moment arrived recently, and June came out straight, asked Maggie if she was over Arthur. Maggie said she was.

Maggie said she was! Libby's heart skips. She eyes the wine bottle, solitary in the rack beside the fireplace.

Better news follows. To help Maggie over her loss, there's a doctor at the hospital where she and June work. Handsome, rich, and avid in his pursuit of Nurse Greene. Maggie, June tells Libby, is going this weekend to the doctor's birthday party at his parents' big house.

Libby's eyes race to the top of the page. She checks the letter's date. The party is tonight. She hugs herself, imagining the handsome doctor sweeping a delighted Maggie off her feet and into his arms. Lucky girl! Folding the letter, Libby slips it into its envelope and stands to collect the wine, a glass and the corkscrew.

⋄⋄⋄⋄⋄

Maggie stares through the taxi window as the vehicle leaves the main roads and enters the quiet, tree-lined streets of the prestigious suburb, a few minutes' walk to the city across parkland dotted with oaks planted a century ago. The houses are tall, old, gracious, and largely hidden behind

The Past can Wait

high brick walls and clipped hedges.

The urge to ask the driver to turn around and take her home suffuses Maggie like a panic attack. What on earth is she thinking? Is a dress all she needs to make her fit in?

'You're a right stunner, love,' her mother said when Maggie slipped into the smoky haze of the living room to seek approval before venturing into the night. 'Our own Cinderella.' Nancy stubbed out her cigarette and squinted at her daughter, head to the side, nodding her satisfaction.

Her father peered over his newspaper. 'Always a princess to me, Mags. You could wear a sack and be beautiful as far as I'm concerned.'

Maggie groaned. 'Lovely, Dad, although not helpful.'

'You'll outshine the lot,' he clarified. Maggie had to make do with that.

Her mother had surprised her with her purchase at a city department store. Under the admiring gaze of her parents, Maggie stroked the deep red taffeta of the dress. A full skirt to a whisper below the knees, a narrow waist, boat neck and three quarter sleeved, the simple gown fitted the slimmer Maggie like a glove.

'Hang on,' her mother said. 'Come with me.'

Nancy strode into her bedroom, Maggie trailing behind. Her mother buried her head in her wardrobe and wriggled out bearing aloft a tissue-wrapped package which she unfolded with a triumphant, 'Knew I'd kept it. Bought it for your brother's wedding in a mad moment, hoping to cheer me up, and never wore it.'

She handed Maggie a silky white stole patterned with delicate red roses. 'For when it cools, later.'

Maggie recalled the deep scarlet, almost black dress her silently disapproving mother wore for Teddy and Raine's rushed wedding five years ago. This delicate piece of flummery worn by the groom's mother would have been out of place. A mad moment indeed. One which would now pay off.

Staring at the passing houses, Maggie calms her panic. Her mother hit the nail on the head with the Cinderella comparison. Swap the pumpkin coach for the luxury of a taxi, add a frock which makes Maggie feel a million quid, set Luke Elliott up as Prince Charming, and Nancy's cat-that-got-the-cream smirk isn't far-fetched.

'Here we are.' The taxi driver stops at tall gates opening onto a gravelled drive which curves to the left. He peers into the rearview mirror. 'Want me to drive up to the house?'

A muttered yes, and Maggie gives up her last chance to wriggle out of the venture. She unclasps her newly manicured fingers, entwined on her lap, and waits for Prince Charming's castle to come into view. The drive isn't long. The taxi pulls up beside stone steps leading to a wrought-iron decorated verandah. A wide front door stands open to allow a couple to move inside. They hand their coats to a man standing at the entrance.

Maggie raises a quizzical eyebrow. There is a butler?

She pays for the taxi from the small purse in her clutch bag and lets herself out, experiencing a pang of disappointment when the driver doesn't rush to open her door. No one is around to see her grand arrival in any case.

Another couple appear from the corner of the house. There must be parking for cars there. They nod a greeting, and the dinner-suited man gives a small bow and a wave to indicate Maggie should go ahead of them, which she does. As she has no coat to hand over, she smiles at the butler and continues past him.

Music and voices flow from a room at the end of a long tile-patterned passage with a faded runner along its centre. Solid, dark wood hall tables line the passage, each flaunting a luxurious display of blue hydrangea, yellow roses and white lilies set among lush sprays of green foliage. Gilt-framed mirrors and dark landscapes of English countryside fill the spaces between the tables. The smell is of lilies, roses, and expensive perfumes.

The Past can Wait

When Maggie was small, before the war, her grandmother took her to a museum in London. Probably the V&A. The vast rooms with their high ceilings and long walls packed with statues, portraits and displays overwhelmed her. She hated the way the ponderous magnificence made her feel tiny, diminished, of no account. In this over-elaborate hall, the same feeling rises within her. She puts a hand to her silky wrap. If this is merely the hall, what will the party room do to her?

Maggie's courage fails. She twists about to flee the house, and collides with a young woman patting her chestnut pixie-cut hair in front of one of the mirrors. The woman yelps.

'Sorry, sorry,' Maggie stutters. Heat rises in her cheeks. 'Realised I've left something–'

'You're here!' Luke bears down on the two of them. He holds a full champagne glass in one hand and smiles as if Maggie's arrival is all he ever wanted, birthday or no birthday.

Maggie's eyes widen at the gorgeous vision the doctor presents. He's wearing a white shirt with white bow tie, fashionably slightly baggy trousers, and a matching wide-lapelled jacket which cinches tight at the waist. His buttonhole sports a yellow rose.

'I see you've met my sister, Veronica.' He pats the young woman's shoulder with his free hand. 'Your hair is fine, Ronnie. Your own problem if you don't like that short cut.'

Veronica scowls. 'Of course I like it. I'm the twin of Audrey Hepburn.' She attempts a look of mysterious glamour in imitation of the actress, and Maggie holds in an unbidden giggle.

Luke rolls his eyes. 'Go and see to our guests. Pull your weight for a change and help Mother out. I'll be there in a moment.'

Veronica raises her eyebrows at Maggie, her red lips pursed, self-admonishing. 'Bossy big brothers,' she mutters. Chin tilted high, she wanders slowly towards the music and voices. As she enters the room at the end, she casts a last, long glance at Maggie over her shoulder.

Luke holds out the champagne, and Maggie takes it reflexively. Without the distraction of the sister, she can't help stare openly at the sophisticated picture her host presents. The lift of one corner of Luke's mouth, Clark Gable style, tells her he's aware of her appraisal. He eyes her in return, from the tips of her white satin shoes (June's wedding shoes, borrowed) to the top of her swept-up hair.

'You are more than beautiful tonight, Nurse Greene. You must only dance with me, I command it.' He makes a small bow and offers Maggie his arm. 'Let's introduce you to the less ferocious of the tribe, shall we?'

Maggie's fingers rest on Luke's arm. When she draws in a small breath to control her fluttering nerves, she tastes crisp linen, expensive wool, and a manly aftershave. She prepares to enjoy herself.

◇◇◇◇◇

'Tell me you danced the night away with your Prince Charming, and need to beg my forgiveness for losing one of my wedding shoes when you fled at midnight–' June adds drama to the last phrase with a breathy voice and uplifted hands '–and at this very moment Dr Elliott is scouring the hospital, ward by ward, searching for his mysterious princess.'

'Whom he won't find.' Maggie slumps further into the wooden bench. She blows out her cheeks in a petulant puff.

June drove around mid-morning in her new Volkswagen to collect the wedding shoes (two). As neither of them had work that day, June urged a drive to the beach, 'so you can fill me in on every minute'.

The weather has cooled after the last two mild days, and Maggie wears a woollen jacket and warm trousers. She has packed a thermos and cheese sandwiches into a holdall, and she and June sit on a bench, sunshine and clouds overhead, with a view of the blue waters of the gulf. Seagulls scream for their share of the bread and cheese, wheeling overhead in a grey and white flurry of raucous demands. Maggie ignores them.

'Okay.' June pours milky coffee into the lid of the thermos and offers it to Maggie, who shakes her head. 'What happened? Whatever it was hasn't restored you to your normal lively self.'

'It was awful.' Maggie's stomach churns, re-living her humiliation.

'How was it awful? Were people rude to you?' June sips the coffee.

'Not openly.' Maggie tosses a scrap of bread crust to the sand and watches half a dozen gulls battle for it. She empathises with the crust, torn apart by sharp, uncaring beaks. 'Luke was all right. Big welcome, told me I looked fabulous–'

'I bet you did,' June murmurs.

Maggie shrugs. 'And he introduced me as a friend he'd met recently, one of the country's new English immigrants.' She faces June. 'They were pleasant enough at first, asking about being in London in the war, and too many sordid questions about the Blitz.' She snorts. 'Never had a scare in their lives, or a day without sleeping in their own beds or not knowing where their next meal's coming from. Spoiled, soft.'

'Well…' June pours out the dregs of her coffee and screws the cap in place. 'At least they were interested in you.'

'Yeah, like a freak show.' Maggie flings the remains of her sandwich to the snatching gulls. 'Turned nasty when they asked how I knew Luke, and I said, all innocent, I was a nurse at the Royal and we worked together.'

'Ah.' June scratches her scalp through her blonde curls. 'They assumed you were a run-of-the-mill doctor chaser …?'

'One of Luke's friends,' Maggie spits it out with sudden fury, 'dared to joke to him about how he'd'– she adopts a posh accent –'attracted a terribly pretty one this time and good on you old boy for letting her catch you.'

'No.'

'Yes.'

'What did Luke say?'

'He said how lucky he was, and then, bless him, told the guy, deadpan, it had been the other way around, he'd had to chase me.'

'Bet that shut them up.'

Maggie blows a soft raspberry into the wind. 'In front of me, yes. It didn't shut them up otherwise.'

'No, I guess they would've gossiped privately.'

'And too loudly.' Having begun venting her fury, Maggie wants to finish it. There might be solace in getting this off her chest.

June brushes crumbs from her skirt and gives Maggie a questioning arch of her eyebrows.

'I excused myself,' Maggie says, 'let them think I was searching for the loo.' She stares ahead at the gently breaking waves spreading their lacy froth on the wet sand. The clouds have won their battle with the sun, and the afternoon is cooling. 'I heard my name, and someone laughing, as I passed one of the rooms. Probably a library.' She sneers the word.

The overheard conversation is seared on her brain, and her heart.

'That accent,' a woman said. 'How can Luke listen to those dropped aitches and not laugh out loud?'

High-pitched giggles, over which someone else chimed in with, 'How could he toss poor Cecily over for his own Eliza Doolittle?'

'Maybe he plans to turn her into a princess.' More merriment. 'She's thrilled, of course. Got her doctor on the hook, or thinks she does.'

A gentler voice burst in, admonishing. One Maggie recognised. 'She's pretty, and nice too. She doesn't deserve you being horrible. Think what she's lived through. You're all awful.'

'Dear Veronica, ever rooting for the underdog.' Laughter.

And Veronica snapping, 'Poor girl, I hope big brother doesn't play with her too long. I like her. I'd be her friend.'

'And then I left,' Maggie says. 'I made sure to find his mother first, thanked her for a lovely party, told her what a splendid home she had, and I had an early shift and had to be off.'

'How did you get home?'

'Walked into the city to the taxi rank. The whole night cost a king's ransom and made me miserable.'

June reaches out with a sympathetic pat of Maggie's arm. 'Poor girl.'

She offers nothing further, and Maggie is grateful for the lack of advice. She takes the thermos from June and tucks it into the holdall. The remaining scraps of sandwiches are flung to the seagulls, which squabble with a vicious intensity to match Maggie's roiling mood. She's waded into deep, shark-infested waters, far from the sparkling calm she and Arthur mostly enjoyed. How far out can she go, does she wish to go, before the sharks have her for dinner?

'I should have said no, right off.' She gazes out at the eternal roll of the waves before turning to June with a grimace. 'Including to that damn play right at the beginning.'

Chapter Ten

SINCE THE VISIT TO THE farm, Arthur hasn't seen Libby. Dealing with the people of Adaminaby in planning the town's relocation next year is an intense process. While the distance is short, the emotional effect is understandably huge.

Gardens, for example, can't be moved. That doesn't stop several keen gardeners telling him they plan to dig up favourite shrubs and beds of bulbs to replant, and will the Authority pay for the cost of the pots to transport them in? Arthur's days fill with questions and problems. It doesn't matter how small they are, each takes time to resolve.

As the evenings close in towards winter, he returns to the boarding house, eats whatever Mrs Carter has left warming in the oven, and falls into bed.

Neither has he had much to do with Kurt Vogel. They see each other regularly in the small office and exchange courteous hellos, how's it going? Most business matters are dealt with by Kurt's team, and the finance man retains his aloof, competent reputation beyond that small group.

Arthur wonders if he dreamed the night at Easter when they shared a bottle of schnapps and Kurt revealed his own war and its tragedy. Is the German sorry he did so? Like Arthur's embarrassment at spilling his sorrows to Libby the first night he returned to the mountains. Unfounded, given Arthur went on to tell her more of his life's woes.

Kurt has no reason to be sorry for his confidences. Arthur is humbled to have been the listener. Or does the man not remember, his brain fogged with schnapps? One day, when life is less hectic, Arthur will invite Kurt to share another drink. Not schnapps.

There are nights when Arthur's over-tired brain insists on spinning in place like a tyre in mud. At these times, he gets out of bed, shoves his arms into his heavy wool dressing gown and his feet into sheepskin slippers, and

The Past can Wait

creeps stealthily to the kitchen to make tea.

Some nights, he doesn't return to his room. He takes his hot drink to the shared sitting room and sits in the light of the moon coming through the window, letting his thoughts romp to a hoped-for exhaustion. They are not all thoughts about pots for shrubs, or organising the timetable of flatbed trucks to cart off whole houses, or assuring a hysterical woman that the churchyard where her parents and sister are buried will not be drowned by the spreading lake. He has pinned a large map to the wall on the public side of the counter and invites the many with concerns to study it and learn where the watery boundary will be.

He knows how they feel. He lost his home too. He works hard to assure the worriers that the future is solid, its foundations laid, and can't they appreciate the benefits? Running hot water and indoor toilets.

These are the main conversations which clog his brain. They are not the only ones. He recites his last conversation with Maggie, nearly six months ago in the airless heat of New Year's Eve. In his tiredness, regret lodges in his gut, threatens him with tears.

He was too hasty, too forceful. He should have led her to the idea more gently, paused to examine it from her side as he examines the townspeople's fears. He should have written to her. He should have called her. Said he was sorry he broke it to her like that, and could he come home and they would talk about it and find another way? Because he misses her with a dull ache which long working days won't dispel.

Alf's warnings, when Arthur visited in March, rattle in his brain. 'A word to the wise,' his friend said. 'There's a doctor, at the Royal. Handsome, rich, and dead keen on our Maggie.'

He's left it too late. What chance does he have now? This well-heeled doctor has slipped into Maggie's life with his money and his doubtless suave manners, and Maggie will have forgotten Arthur and his stupid plans and house obsession.

On these nights, Arthur finishes his tea, takes the cup to the kitchen, washes and dries it. He slips into his bed, pulls the bedspread to his neck and closes his eyes. When his travel clock jangles its alarm, he knows exhaustion claimed him at some point, because he wakes with a jolt, groaning, unwilling to face the day.

◇◇◇◇◇

Luke catches Maggie as she walks one drizzly evening out of the hospital's main entrance on her way to the bus stop.

'Maggie, wait up. Can I have a word, please?'

She halts by the door and turns to him. He's wearing a coat, and has either just arrived or is leaving, as she is. His hair is dry. He's leaving. Maggie waits, stiff backed, for him to approach, squashing the humiliation of the night of the party.

'You left on Saturday without saying goodbye,' Luke says. He stands close, and Maggie takes a step away. 'I went searching. None of my friends said they'd seen you–'

'I thanked your mother.' Anger rises in her gorge. 'Contrary to what your *friends* think, manners belong to everyone.' She clenches her teeth, mutters, 'Not just posh nobs with their pools and tennis courts.'

Luke blinks at the onslaught. 'I was about to add, except Mother.' He gives a slight nod. 'Who told me you're delightful, a breath of fresh air were her words. And made of sterner stuff than, quote, all your twittering friends put together, dear.' His smile is broad.

A middle-aged woman helps an old man through the door. Both wear raincoats. The woman's permed, bleached hair is spotted with moisture, as is the old man's hat. Maggie steps aside to let them pass. The woman mouths a thanks.

Maggie returns her gaze to Luke. She's not flattered by Mrs Elliott's condescending praise, an improvement though it is over what others said about her. 'Well, good. Then you know,' Maggie says in a voice tight with emotion, 'I needed to leave early.'

'Why?' He wears his puzzlement like a child, open, questioning. 'You told her you had an early shift. You didn't. I checked, before the party.'

Maggie goes on the attack. 'I caught a conversation not meant for my ears.' She shifts the canvas holdall carrying her purse, her nurses' shoes and cap and other odds and ends, from one hand to the other. 'I can tell when I'm not welcome.'

'Not welcome …?' Luke's eyes take on a hard gleam. 'What happened? Who said what?'

Two nurses rush past, buttoning their coats, chatting, glad to be out of there. They have umbrellas tucked under their arms and they stop at the door to unfurl them. One looks curiously at Maggie and Luke, casts a raised eyebrow to her friend.

'This isn't the place to talk,' Maggie says. 'It doesn't matter anyway. I need to go or I'll miss my bus. Can't afford to take taxis everywhere.' She gives a thin-lipped smile and pivots on her heel to leave.

Luke clasps her sleeve. 'Don't go,' he says. 'I was leaving too. Why don't I drive you home, you can tell me what this is about—'

'No thank you.' Maggie lifts his fingers from her arm. 'It's been nice. See you around.'

He lets her leave. 'Please, can we at least talk, soon?' he calls. 'When do you have your next day off? Please, Maggie.'

Maggie pushes at the door, face averted from his entreaties. She digs into the holdall for her rain bonnet, opens its pleats, clamps it on her curls and ties the clear plastic straps under her chin. Her hair will be wild enough with the damp. She doesn't want to scare her fellow bus travellers, looking like a mad woman.

Rushing along the Terrace, skirting puddles where the rain, heavier now, fractures the reflected light of the streetlamps, Maggie holds Luke's puzzlement and his seeming outrage in her mind. He checked on her shifts. Before the party. He expected her to stay, have fun, not dash off at midnight, glass slipper or not. These musings go some way to mollifying her rage.

On the bus, Maggie peers through the rain-streaked glass as city streets give way to the main road, the bell buzzing for frequent stops. Her anger might have waned, but her weariness, the weather, the early darkness, work to bolster her dark mood.

She misses Arthur. Her pain for his loss blossoms anew, filling her body as she sits there on the bus. There's no gentle knocking to let itself in, this ache she hoped would have settled, locked behind her ribs. If Arthur wrote to her, or rang … He hasn't. Nothing in five months. He's taken her at her word, let her choose her path. With no argument.

Maggie wriggles in the seat, remembering June's early suggestions that Maggie could always get her engagement ring back. Stubbornness stayed her hand from letter or telephone. Arthur was the one being unreasonable, forever delaying. She huffs out a breath, working through her feelings, searching for clues about Arthur's feelings. His obsession about the house was an excuse, covering his uncertainty about their future together. Maggie's burst of temper on New Year's Eve had been her unconscious doubts exploding with the sudden fury of Vesuvius.

Another passenger rings the bell for Maggie's stop. She resets her rain bonnet, slides from the seat, clutching the holdall and swaying with the motion of the bus while she braces herself for the stop.

'Goodnight,' she tells the driver as she steps to the footpath. He responds with a 'Take care, love.' His northern English accent is strong.

The other passenger who alights is a woman, about Maggie's age. A man in a trench coat, holding a black umbrella, waits in the bus shelter to meet her. They kiss

The Past can Wait

their greeting and hurry off into the rain, huddled under the umbrella. Maggie tightens the plastic bow at her chin and walks after them, envying their comfortable togetherness.

Arthur is gone from her life. Another man wants to be part of it. One who won't take no so easily. Does she need to give Luke another chance? How he reacted in the hospital entrance suggests he's not like his friends. And maybe not all his friends are like those she overheard. Luke's sister, Veronica, stuck up for Maggie, told the others off, said she'd be Maggie's friend.

If Luke searches her out, asks to talk, Maggie will say yes. She trudges through the cold rain, following the yellow streetlamps to home. Her decision does nothing to ease her aching heart.

Chapter Eleven

'LETTER FOR YOU, ARTHUR.' MRS Carter walks out of the dining room and points to the white envelope on the hall telephone table. 'Dinner at six,' she adds, heading to the kitchen. 'Nice to have you in for a change.'

'Evening.' Arthur greets her, removing his woollen gloves. He must find his sheepskin pair. Winter hovers on the town's doorstep, eager to advance in the wake of its vanguard of cold, breezy days and near-freezing nights.

'Need a hot meal, starving,' he calls to Mrs Carter. He picks up the letter, recognising Alf's untidy hand, and carries it to his room, switching on the dim overhead light as he enters.

Alf writes occasionally. Very occasionally.

Arthur places the letter on the pine chest of drawers, unbuttons his coat and removes his jacket and tie. He pulls a jumper over his head before exchanging his shoes for slippers. The shoes will go on again for dinner: one of Mrs Carter's rules of civilisation.

The letter worries him. It can't be bad news because Alf would have rung. It can't be about Arthur's family because his mother or father would have called, or written, depending on the emergency.

He pushes aside shirts, socks and trousers garnishing the bedroom chair, and slumps into the worn, deep cushions. The letter remains unopened in his hands. He flips it over, reading the return address and imagining Alf and June this moment at their kitchen table, eating, talking about the day's events – what excitement filled the Royal's wards today, what new housing development Alf will soon be working on, the slow progress of renovation at Teddy and Raine's rambling Victorian terrace by the sea. The old house holds Arthur's attention for a few seconds. Good bones, as Teddy's dad says of the place. Has Raine painted the living room yet, hauling her small body up ladders to

The Past can Wait

reach the cornices eleven feet above her? Arthur has helped with the work on and off, sanding, painting, holding tools and wiring while Alf swears at the ancient electrics, trying to avoid killing himself …

Arthur glances at his watch. Ten minutes to six. More than enough time to open and read a letter. He slits the flap with his fingernail. There are two closely written pages.

Dear Arthur

I was going to ring you, except it seemed too dramatic, like we were in a film. A letter seemed a better idea, not too scary. First, our news. We're well here which is good because, Big Announcement!!!! June and me are going to be parents. What do you think of that? Hard to believe and makes me nervous. Babies are awful small. Guess my practice with Teddy and Raine's two kids might come in useful if I can remember that long ago. June tells me we can expect baby Hall to arrive at the end of September, so I reckon it was that New Year's Party which is to blame! June will give up work sometime in the winter. She says she'd like to go back to nursing when baby is old enough, and I guess we'll need the money! As well as being small, I believe kids also cost a lot, at least that's what Teddy says!!

Arthur lays the letter on his knees and grins his delight. If anyone is cut out to be Dad of the Year, it's Alf. The time Teddy ran away, hiding out up here in the mountains at Guthega, Alf stood in as surrogate dad to baby Stevie and helped Raine out as much as she'd let him. Arthur's grin widens. Not that it did Alf any good. Raine wasn't interested in any romance with Alf, despite the fact he worshipped the ground she trod on. Her heart, for better or worse – and many would say worse – was with Teddy. Arthur sighs. Despite all the drama, life has turned out fine for them all.

The second page of the letter waits to be read. Arthur pulls it from behind the first sheet and reads, slowly, taking it in.

That's us. Aside from telling you our good news, I feel I should tell you, as a friend, that things with Maggie on the doctor front are warming up. A couple of weeks ago, Maggie went to the guy's birthday party at his parents' posh mansion in North Adelaide (the other half, hey?). June told me she thought Maggie might give the doctor – his name's Luke Elliott – a wide berth after. Something happened to upset her, I gather. Anyway, all is forgiven as they're an item, off to see the latest films, visits to art galleries, dinners out. June is happy for Maggie. I'm not sure. June's known her less than a year, and she doesn't know you from Adam. Mags keeps losing weight, which isn't a good sign, is it? Women think they have to be skinny these days, so it could be that. Having to fit into fancy new frocks.

It's up to you, mate. You might've found yourself a new love in the mountains (it can happen, ha ha!), and it's truly over with Mags. If that's the case, ignore this bit of the letter and just be pleased for me and June and our new Big Adventure!

Yours sincerely,

Alf

A broiling waterfall of emotions flood Arthur's head, chest and stomach, tumbling into the aching void which opened inside him when Maggie stormed off on New Year's Eve. Grief is there, together with a deep sense of loneliness, of abandonment and hopelessness. And, he confesses, jealousy.

He captures the jealousy, sensing this is a feeling he can do something about. It's not that he's jealous of the doctor – well, of course he is, imagining this good-looking man holding Maggie, taking her hand … he won't let himself picture them kissing.

More than the man himself, is what this doctor can give Maggie. Everything she wants. A house, which Arthur is sure will be more than the bog standard three bedroom bungalow on a new housing estate which he'd considered. Museums, theatre, dinners in expensive restaurants. Security and ease in which to raise a family.

He crumples the letter in his fist, and bends forward, head in his hands. How stupid he's been, not insisting on talking right from the troubled start, in January, before this fellow came on the scene. He can't now. Maggie would mock him, and with good reason. Arthur has less to offer her than he did before.

'Arthur. You coming to eat, love?' Mrs Carter's cautious knock on his door pulls him from his self-chastising.

While his appetite has fled, Arthur hauls himself from the cushions, dropping the letter in his waste paper basket. 'On my way,' he says.

He forgets to swap his slippers for shoes. In the small, over-decorated dining room, Mrs Carter peers down, frowns, and opens her mouth. Arthur waits for the ticking off and receives instead a quiet, 'Hope there wasn't bad news in that letter.'

'No, no.' He sits at his place. 'Smells delicious, Mrs C, thanks.'

Arthur wades through a near acceptable proportion of the too-large serving of beef stew. He's constantly reminding his landlady he doesn't work in the tunnels, he has an office job and he doesn't need as much food as she believes. She ignores him. This evening, she doesn't complain when he fails to clear his plate and refuses sweets.

Two temporary guests who have joined them for the meal decide their fellow lodger isn't the talkative kind and, after initial enquiries, retreat to chatting with each other. As soon as it's remotely polite, Arthur returns to his room. He will play a record or two, make notes for what he has to do at work tomorrow, distract himself, if he can.

He selects the Harptones' melancholy 'Life is But a Dream' from the meagre pile on the chest of drawers, and removes the single from its sleeve. He's placing the vinyl disc on the turntable when the telephone in the hall trills its urgency.

Mrs Carter answers testily, too late for people to be ringing in her view. Her voice changes on learning the identity of the caller. 'I'll fetch him, love, won't be a tick,' she says, kindly.

Arthur waits for the knock on his door. His heart thuds.

The call must be for him. Wild dreams spin in his brain. Maggie is desperate to see him. Life has gone sour with the fancy doctor, she's sorry, she misses him. Can he come home? Can she come up there? They need to talk …

'It's Libby, Arthur, ringing from Cooma,' Mrs Carter says through the door.

Libby.

Disappointment punctures his moment of exhilaration, his moroseness settling like dust after an explosion.

'I …' He wants to say, 'Tell her I've gone out.'

'Arthur, it's not polite to keep a lady waiting.'

Politeness will be Arthur's undoing. 'I'm coming.' He slides 'Life is But a Dream' into its sleeve.

◈◈◈◈◈

Libby has searched for an excuse to ring Arthur since she received June's letter a couple of weeks ago. In the nearly two months which have passed since the outing to her parents', their single contact has been a thank you note Arthur sent care of the hospital. The note, devoid of any mention of further get-togethers, made Libby reluctant to be the initiator until she'd heard from June. Now that she has, and her way is clear to win Arthur's heart, she has needed a valid reason to call.

She has one.

Libby is settled on the sofa with a blanket around her shoulders – a cosy precaution against the cold night air outside. The heavy black phone rests in her lap. A log in the fire collapses into the coals, sending up a shower of red and gold sparks like a mini bonfire on Guy Fawkes night.

'Hello, Libby, what can I do for you?'

Libby frowns into the receiver. Arthur's voice is flat, lacking any warmth. His question makes her feel like she's on a business call. Her usual confidence falters. This is a mistake. He doesn't want to talk to her. She breathes in, draws warmth into her voice.

'Nothing,' she says brightly. 'You've done more than

enough, and we're all grateful.' A clever touch, that 'all'. Keeps it from being too personal.

There's a moment's silence before Arthur mutters, 'Glad I could help *someone*.'

Libby has a lightbulb moment. His brusqueness is nothing to do with her.

'Is everything all right, Arthur?' Concern flows through her voice.

A longer silence, the sound of swallowing. Is he crying?

'Arthur.' Her voice is soft, cajoling, like coaxing a motherless lamb to feed from a bottle. 'What's wrong? Can I help?'

When he answers, he's stronger, like he's made a decision. 'It's fine, Libby.' His laugh is ragged. 'You do have a knack for finding me when I need cheering up. Thank you for that.'

'Glad I could cheer you up, although you haven't told me–'

'No, not your problem.' Arthur gently steers her from her question. 'It's good to hear your voice, and my apologies for ignoring you this long. We did say we'd see each other at some stage, right?'

'Yes, yes.' Libby's curiosity retreats. Her confidence revives itself to march into the vacancy. Here's her opening. 'I have just the occasion.' Her cheeriness is genuine. 'I called because Mum and Dad are celebrating signing the contract on their new home, here in Cooma, one of Peter Adams' places – you probably never met him, he and June went out together, before Alf …' She stops, breathes. 'Sorry, I'm rambling.'

'You are, but never mind.' Arthur's voice is steadier. 'You're right, I never did meet him. Alf told me a bit. The man whose wife everyone assumed had run out on him?'

'That's the one.' Libby prefers not to dwell on those days, and what came afterwards. She soldiers on. 'Irrelevant, shouldn't have mentioned it.' She waves her hand, despite

Arthur being unable to see this. 'What I'm saying in a long-winded way is that Mum and Dad are having a small party at the Australia Hotel this weekend and you're invited.' She giggles. 'Mum specifically told me, and I quote, to make sure that nice young man from the Authority comes along. You see, you can't say no.'

She waits for hesitation. There is none.

'That's kind, and I'm honoured. Tell your mother I'll be there, and congratulations on the house purchase.'

Libby gives him the details, tells him it will be suit and tie, and there'll be a crowd given her parents are friends with the whole area.

And then she asks, casually, 'And work and life are going well? Any news from home?'

The silence returns, an instant of palpable gloom. 'June's going to have a baby,' Arthur blurts. 'Isn't that great?' He makes a weird noise, like a muffled snort. 'You probably already knew.'

'Yes, yes of course, great news.' Libby hides her hurt. Why didn't June tell her? She struggles to find a positive reason. Likely, she decides glumly, it's because her and June's correspondence is as businesslike as Arthur's question at the beginning of the call.

When she herself is going to be a mother, Libby decides, she'll announce it to the world, so no one feels left out. Once, that is, she's found the father of this future child.

There's little left to say. Libby takes pity on Arthur, gaily insisting it's past her bedtime, but she wanted to catch him this evening, make sure he would come, and they say goodbye, see you in a few days, and Arthur hangs up with a gentle click.

Libby sets the receiver in its cradle and decides her parents' gathering is a great reason for a new frock.

The Past can Wait

Chapter Twelve

THE AIR IS DRY AND too cold for this part of the world. Maggie is glad of the blanket over her knees as Luke drives up into the hills above the city. Mist wavers between the trees, the birds are silent, and traffic is sparse on this early Sunday morning. Veronica, who has been as good as her word and befriended Maggie, dozes on the rear seat.

They approach a stony farm track on their right, heading steeply up the hillside and lined with tall red gums. Maggie's sure it's the track leading to Raine and Teddy's tiny cabin, their first home of their own, and which Raine professes to miss to this day. Maggie half-turns, points, asking if Luke noticed the road, telling him her brother and sister-in-law once lived in a shack up there.

'Better them than me,' Luke says. 'The countryside is pleasant enough for a day out, but I wouldn't want to live there.'

'You wouldn't fancy being a country GP?' Maggie says. A fleeting image of herself as the GP's wife, with the status the position would bring in a small town, presents itself in her mind. She examines it, unsure of the appeal.

'No, thank you.' Luke laughs. 'What on earth would you do outside surgery hours?'

Maggie has no idea. How *do* people entertain themselves in these small towns? Like Adaminaby, for example. Arthur seems to find enough to keep him occupied. She papers over the sadness which refuses to budge from its firm hold inside her ribcage by silently scolding her former fiancé for his lack of contact. Six months, and no word except the occasional, and uninteresting, bit of gossip via June. Maggie knows only that Arthur is busy with the wholesale moving of the town to make way for a great big dam.

'Are we nearly there yet?' Veronica's sleepy voice drifts from the rear seat.

'Not too far,' Luke says, which is an ambiguous answer.

They crest the low hills and wind their way to flatter country. On the plains, out of the wooded mists, the cold is curbed by bright sunshine. Lush green fields spread to the distance.

Maggie is apprehensive about this outing.

'Off to an old winery,' Luke told her a few days ago. 'Owned since the dawn of time by a schoolmate's family. Going strong despite wars and depressions.'

Maggie is not a wine drinker and is unsure of the purpose of this outing. Will they drink the wine? Or learn how it's made, like a school trip? She determines to relax, to enjoy the time off from work and the city, and to not let her ignorance worry her.

Her apprehension is not eased when they arrive and pull up in front of a low, long stone homestead where purplish-pink flowers cover a bullnosed verandah. White smoke curls into the air from a multi-pot chimney. It's not the homestead which causes concern. A group of people gathered in the driveway wave enthusiastically as Luke steps out of the car. Maggie recognises them from the birthday party. Two are strangers – a couple, judging by the way the woman is draped along the length of the man's side.

Veronica crouches over from the rear seat, touches Maggie's shoulder. 'Don't let the bastards grind you down,' she whispers. 'Stick with me, you'll be fine.' She assesses the people, bundled in coats and hats. 'Oh dear,' she murmurs. 'Our Cecily is here.'

Maggie is about to ask who Cecily is when the name jolts her already on high alert brain. Luke's former girlfriend. The one Maggie overheard a woman at the party whiningly ask how Luke could have given her up for the doctor-snatching nurse.

She peers more closely at the unfamiliar couple, or rather, at the woman. Cecily is petite, slim, with fashionable short curly hair. Her tailored long coat is open to reveal dark, well-cut trousers and a fitted green top, both of which display her figure at its best. The coat is red, perfectly matching her lipstick, and her eyes are heavily made up to accentuate their wide gaze. Maggie decides Cecily is either a film star or a model. Glamour oozes from her. The man's arm wraps her waist.

With a muted smirk, Cecily watches Luke make his way to the passenger side of the car.

'She's beautiful,' Maggie says to Veronica. But her friend has clambered from the car and is moving towards the group, holding out her arms for embraces and pecks on the cheek. When she gets to Cecily, the embrace is punctilious, on both sides.

Maggie stiffens, anticipating contempt. She wishes she were far away. She wants to click the car lock into place and plead a headache, say she'll stay where she is.

Luke opens the door and offers Maggie his hand. A hint of anxiety clouds his eyes.

'I had no idea Cecily was coming,' he says. 'Bit of history there.' He turns all jolly, saying, 'Good to see she has a new man in her life. Cecily can't be without one.' His laugh is strained.

Taking a deep breath, Maggie pats her messy curls. Ensuring her own coat is buttoned to disguise her plain skirt and bulky jumper, she emerges from the car. Veronica walks to her, takes her hand and leads her forward to re-introduce her to the chatting gathering.

Bless Veronica. Maggie strives for confidence. The day might be fun, possibly.

Cecily is polite, bordering on warmth, when Luke makes the introductions. The new man introduces himself as Nick, with Cecily adding for the benefit of the gathering that Nick works for Elders – 'Oldest property company in the state,' as an aside to Maggie, who has no idea – and has recently bought a 'a bit of agricultural land for himself'.

'Thinking of going into wine making, like this place,' Nick volunteers. 'Mark my words, in the future the whole region will be given over to grapes. Best be in at the bottom, hey?'

Luke overrides Veronica's giggles at the mention of bottoms to agree it's wise of Nick.

'Which is why we gate-crashed your outing today.' Cecily fixes Luke with a steely stare, daring him not to be welcoming.

Maggie watches the back and forth, stifling her own giggle. Nick and Cecily seem perfect for each other. What had Luke seen in her, with her airs and pretensions? Apart from a beautiful face and a sophistication to match the house in North Adelaide.

She stifles the thought and concentrates on the tour, making mental notes to impress June and Alf, and Teddy and Raine when they next meet. From where the grapes are unloaded to the point at which the wine is bottled and crated, Maggie finds it fascinating, especially the old wine press, built in 1892 and still in working order.

Luke's friend, a son of the winery owner, exudes enthusiasm and answers Nick's endless questions with endless answers. Leaving Nick to finish his quizzing, and Luke to say thank you, the group wanders to a cloth-covered trestle table set up by the big doors. Another brother stands here with half a dozen open dark green bottles and a collection of tiny glasses.

Maggie is thirsty. She takes an offered glass, raises it to her lips, and tips the contents into her mouth. The velvety ruby liquid slides down satisfyingly.

'That's lovely–' She stops.

Six pairs of eyes stare at her. Five pairs dance with glee. Three women hold their hands to their mouths, poorly hiding their grins.

'Oh dear me.' Cecily's clear voice rings out. 'Dear Luke should really house train his little conquests before setting them loose in polite company.'

Veronica, whose eyes hold only embarrassment, scowls

ferociously at Cecily and rushes to Maggie's side. Turning to the tittering women and openly grinning men, she scolds, '*You* had to be taught what to do, didn't you? Which bloody knife and fork to use, tasting wines, polite conversation … all of it.'

Maggie stands frozen, the glass in her hand as heavy and as dangerous as a grenade without its pin. She has no idea what she has done wrong. She does know that Veronica's well-meaning defence makes her wish the old flagstone floor would crack from one end to the other and suck her into its oblivious depths.

It's the mortification of the party replayed in living colour. Worse, because this time she's brought it on herself, somehow, and can't pretend she's ignorant of the scorn. If she could turn her back on them and walk home, she would.

'What's happening?' Luke is there, thunder in his face. 'What did you say, Cecily?'

'Me?' Cecily curls her red lips into a grin. 'Not a word, Luke dear.' She waves a dismissive hand at Maggie, keeps her mocking smile going. 'So sorry, Maggie – it is Maggie, right? Not Margaret or Meg? – one shouldn't find it funny.' She tips her head at Veronica, gracious in the extreme. 'Your bulldog sister here is right, Luke dear. One has to be taught correct behaviours, growing up. My apologies.'

Maggie drags her voice from under its humiliation. 'No problem,' she says, hating the tremor in her words. 'It would help if someone explained what I did wrong.' She lifts the corners of her mouth. She will be a good sport, she will not let them see her embarrassment, she will not be angry. Dignity is her byword. 'To avoid future mistakes.'

'You explain, you're her *friend*.' Cecily sends the dismissive wave Veronica's way, and talks to Luke. 'We must run, dinner tonight with Nick's parents, mustn't be late.' She hesitates, leans in like she plans to kiss him on the cheek and thinks better of it in the face of his hostile stare. 'Thanks for letting us tag along. Enjoy the rest of your day.' Turning on her heel, she waggles her fingers at the group and walks with steady precision and the tiniest sway of her bottom towards Nick, still in deep discussion about the finer points of winemaking.

Maggie watches her go. She doesn't dare look anywhere else.

⬦⬦⬦⬦⬦

Mrs Harrington has returned to Maggie's ward. Painfully thin, her parchment skin wrinkled over protruding bones, Maggie is aware her patient is unlikely to leave this time. Mrs Harrington is also aware.

'Home is chaotic,' she says to Maggie. Each word is enunciated with a breath between them.

Maggie fixes pillows and lifts Mrs Harrington into a half-sitting, half-lying position with the ease of handling a small child.

'Chaotic?'

'They come and go constantly, whisper to each other, fuss at all hours.' Mrs Harrington breathes in, out. 'Forever asking me if I need something.' Her lips stretch in a skeletal grin. 'Here, there's a routine.' She slowly lifts a veined hand to pat Maggie's arm. 'And I'm in the best of care.'

'We try our hardest.' There's a lot of coming and going and fussing at all hours in the wards too. Maggie respects Mrs Harrington's bravery and will do her damndest to ensure her positivity is justified.

'Right, Mrs H,' she says. 'While I don't want to sound like your family, can I bring you something? Magazines?'

'No, dear.' Mrs Harrington points to the bedside locker, past a pot of pink cyclamen. 'I have a book in there. If you could fetch that out for me …'

When Maggie passes her the Agatha Christie paperback, Mrs Harrington makes a point of staring at Maggie's left hand, where the white band mark has long since disappeared.

'You haven't made up … with that nice fiancé of yours?'

The Past can Wait

She stares up, frowning.

'How did you know? And why do you think he's nice?' Maggie is certain she never shared the breakup with Mrs Harrington, although that stinking hot January day when the tears welled if anyone asked, however innocently, if she was all right, is branded in her memory. She is moved by the woman remembering her upset, given what's going on in her own life.

'Ah.' Mrs Harrington taps the side of her nose. 'I have ways ...'

Maggie rolls her eyes. Gossiping nurses.

'Then, no,' she says. 'And thank you for asking.' She straightens the water jug, not wanting to appear to be rushing off to avoid further questioning.

'Are you happy, dear?'

The question, rich with genuine concern, brings sudden tears to Maggie's eyes. Happy? Six months on?

'Yes, yes of course,' she stammers. She brings out a smile. 'And I do have other patients I have to take care of.'

Mrs Harrington waves her off. She doesn't return Maggie's smile.

For the next two days, her patient is asleep when Maggie passes by on her rounds, or is surrounded by family during visiting hours. On the third day, mid-morning, she finds the old lady sitting up in bed dressed to the nines in a crisp, pink cotton nightgown and a pink and cream crocheted bed jacket. Maggie hasn't seen either before. Her cheeks have a faint flush to them.

Mrs Harrington puts her Agatha Christie novel on the bed, inserting a bookmark at the two thirds mark, and welcomes Maggie with her usual warmth.

Maggie senses interrogation and is not surprised when Mrs Harrington opens with a direct volley, and no indication she has trouble breathing.

'I understand why you're happy, dear.' Her pale blue eyes glint with humour. 'They tell me you're seeing that lovely Dr

Elliott. I can't be more pleased for you. He's a real charmer.' She pauses, blinks. 'Good doctor too.'

Heat rises in Maggie's cheeks. Seeing the lovely Dr Elliott? What is she to say to this? She takes a breath.

Chapter Thirteen

'ARTHUR.' KURT STANDS BY ARTHUR'S desk.

Arthur stops writing the memo he's composing on behalf of a resident. The elderly long-term inhabitant firmly believes the Authority has vastly undervalued his home on the edge of Adaminaby.

'Lot better than these.' The old man had sneered, gesturing at his neighbours' identical houses.

Arthur has learned not to argue, not to say the neighbours are delighted with their compensation. He will have a valuer delve into it, let him break the news. Who knows? The old codger might be right, and the valuer will discover the windows are made of diamond as opposed to common old glass. The weatherboards could be solid gold, not spotted gum.

The week is at its exhausted end, and Arthur wants to get out of there.

He cannot read the finance man's expression. 'Yes, Kurt?' He worries he's messed up somewhere along the line, promised a costly replacement for, say, a garage full of work tools when the tools could be moved to the new town. 'Is anything wrong?'

The inscrutable expression transforms into a surprised, raised eyebrow and a quirky lift of the corner of Kurt's mouth. 'No, no,' he says. 'I invite you to share more schnapps tonight. End of the work week, we relax?'

'Ah.' Arthur's unease melts. 'I'd like that, except no schnapps, please.' He lifts his gaze to the white ceiling. 'Left me with a bit of a reminder last time, to be honest, and tomorrow I have to catch the bus to Cooma for a gathering in the evening.' He grins. 'I'd like a clear head.'

Kurt laughs. 'We stay with your weak Aussie beer. No problem.'

They are joined in the town's one pub by colleagues from the Authority, some slipping out after an hour, a handful lingering longer, until only Arthur and Kurt remain of the group.

The subtly hostile bartender has the evening off, or has resigned in protest at the types he must serve. His replacement is intent on pulling beers and pouring shots, indifferent to the nationalities and accents of his customers. Kurt makes no comment. Neither does Arthur. Instead, they chat casually about the town's move, mock the slowness of the bureaucracy and declare how glad they both will be when this phase is over.

Neither of them venture into what comes after, what other jobs the Authority has for them. Arthur's mind refuses to go that far into a future which begins to bear a depressing resemblance to his recent past.

At closing time, the bartender rings his bell, calls time. The handful of remaining customers gather coats, gloves and hats to ward off the early winter cold, and wander (or stumble) into the dark street.

Arthur realises he has no idea where Kurt lives. Before he can ask, however, Kurt says, 'I drive you to Cooma tomorrow. Better than taking the bus.' He lightly punches Arthur's arm. 'You sleep longer in the morning, ja?'

'You don't need to drive me.' Arthur's protest is real. He is used to the bus, and he doesn't need to leave until lunchtime. Plenty of time to sleep in.

Kurt waves away the objection. 'I need a short holiday,' he says. 'And I must buy a new coat for winter.' He brushes at his long overcoat, fingering a tear in the pocket. 'Could be mended, I am thinking. A Schneider is what I need.'

'A tailor?' Arthur asks.

'Ja, a Schneider.' Kurt grins and claps Arthur on the upper arm. 'I teach you German, you make my English better.' His eyes light with the mischief Arthur is coming to recognise. 'And I will speak with a Cockney accent, will confuse everyone, hey?'

Which is how Arthur comes to be sitting in Kurt's

The Past can Wait

Holden station wagon, a passenger being ferried to Cooma in more comfort, and more speedily, than the local bus. The one-hour journey is nearly done. Despite its best efforts, the car's heater is no match for the weather, and Arthur is glad of his thick winter jacket. Dark clouds mass on the horizon like an invading army about to march across the wide landscape and further dull its muted brown and grey-green hues. The mountains are already white with snow at their higher peaks.

Arthur never tires of the openness of this land, at any season. When he thinks beyond the day to day of his job, he worries that the power stations and their great pipes, and the flooded valleys where the water will be held at bay by towering concrete walls, will destroy the wildness, the ancient timelessness he has come to love. He's unsure he wants to hang around long enough to see that.

The land here at least, he reminds himself, will remain when the Walters' acres, thousands of others around it, and Adaminaby, are under water. There is consolation in the thought.

When they arrive at the Australia Hotel late morning, Arthur finds a message from Libby.

Please rescue me!!! In the games room blowing up balloons!!

He agrees to meet Kurt for lunch, after the German's search for a tailor, and drops his suit bag and case in his room before seeking Libby out.

'Arthur!' Mrs Walters leaves her half-finished floral arrangement and hurries over to greet him. 'Tom and I are thrilled you could make it.' She beams. 'Lovely of you to come all this way.'

'Wouldn't have missed it for the world.' Arthur returns the beam. 'Congratulations on the house contract.'

'Wonderful, isn't it?' She rolls her eyes. 'Now for the great clear-out. I am *not* looking forward to that, I can tell you.'

Arthur smiles his sympathy and gazes around. 'Libby

left me a note, saying she was blowing up balloons.'

'Gone to the bakery to fetch the cake.' Mrs Walters peers over Arthur's shoulder. 'Here she is.' Her enthusiasm paints Libby as a returned conquering hero.

More greetings, an examination of the cake (triple-tiered, like a wedding cake, iced in mauve with white and lilac decorations), and Mrs Walters tells Libby she has done enough, there's not much left to do, Libby and Arthur should have lunch and entertain themselves for the afternoon. She shoos them out the double doors over Libby's protests, clucking assurances that everything is under control.

They are left standing in the hotel lobby. Arthur shuffles from one foot to the other, suddenly awkward.

'You don't need to 'entertain' me,' he says. 'I'm sure you have things you'd rather be doing.'

'Honestly?' Libby eyes him up and down, grinning. 'A girl gets the chance to spend an afternoon savouring the multiple pleasures of our vast metropolis on the arm of a good-looking gentleman, and she says she'd rather be at home washing her hair?' She giggles, lays a hand on Arthur's arm. 'Come on, I know just the place for lunch.'

'Food sounds great, starving. But – would you mind ...?' He hopes Libby will be okay with this. 'Had a lift from Adaminaby with a mate from the office, and I've said I'll meet him for lunch–'

Libby puts her hands on her hips and frowns. 'You standing me up, Arthur Kaine?'

'God no!' Arthur is mortified. 'I was about to suggest Kurt join us, if that's all right?'

'Sure.' Libby's forehead smooths. 'I guess I can share you for one meal.'

Share him?

They eat at the Italian restaurant. The heavy clouds have made their advance and hang above the town, considering its worth as a conquest. The air is chill, tinged with a dampness Arthur recognises as possible snow. A log burner glows its warmth from one end of the restaurant, and the cosiness encourages them to take their time over lasagna, veal scallopine and ravioli.

Libby questions Kurt about his homeland, keeping to the landscape and how it compares with the Snowy Mountains. Kurt talks about the Alps and skiing in Austria before the war. He has joined the Cooma Ski Club and will be among the first to use the new resort at Guthega this winter.

'Love skiing,' Libby says. 'Dad used to take Rob – my brother,' she explains to Kurt, 'and me every year to Kosciuszko when we were small.' She sets her fork beside her empty plate. 'I haven't been for a few years, sadly. Mum's never been keen, too wet for her. Dad claims he's past it, and when Rob has time he somehow prefers to go with his mates, not his little sister.' She turns to Arthur. 'Are you a skier, Cockney man?'

Arthur pulls a face. 'Sure, skied regularly down Oxford Street. Great fun.'

They laugh, and Libby fixes her green eyes on Kurt. 'Just the two of us then.'

'Talking of snow …' Arthur points to the window with its view to the main street where proof of his earlier suspicions falls from the sky.

Great white flakes drift serenely in the windless air. They sink to the verandahs opposite, the parked cars, and the road, whitening the surfaces briefly before melting.

Libby throws out her hands, palms up. 'Oooh! Lovely!'

'It will not stay,' Kurt says with the tone of one who knows snow.

'Not here it won't, right in town.' Libby waves at the minimal remains of their meals. 'If you've finished, let's go to Nanny Goat Hill, to the lookout,' she says. 'It might settle up there.'

Arthur has heard of Nanny Goat Hill, although he's never been. He pays for their meals over Kurt's objections – 'You saved me a bus fare. Lunch is on me,' he counters –

and Libby leads them along Sharpe Street while the snow falls, more thickly now. A soft white layer accumulates on car roofs. Libby's long legs in their dark corduroy trousers stride ahead of Arthur, her auburn ponytail bouncing on her shoulders in her hurry.

She turns right onto a side street and then left, and begins to climb a steep, unpaved track. Here on the bare earth, the snow has settled. Libby sets a fast pace. Kurt strides beside her. Arthur, panting, wishes he spent less time at his desk as he falls behind.

When he reaches the stone outcrop with its sculptured goat, Kurt and Libby are staring out across the town, through the blur to where the red iron rooftops have paled to pink under their new light covering. The mountains beyond are invisible. There's a wind up here, in this exposed place. It's cold, wild, exhilarating.

Libby greets Arthur with a teasing, 'Slow poke!' She lifts her face to the flakes, arms outstretched like she was basking in sunshine.

Her exuberance is catching, and Arthur impetuously joins her, opening his mouth to capture the cold wetness on his tongue. Kurt views them with tolerance, as if they are over-excited children who need to be indulged. A bubble of happiness climbs from Arthur's stomach into his heart.

'Watch me,' Libby says. 'Haven't done this for years.' She leans into the rock, hands clasping an edge, bending her leg to gain a foothold.

'Be careful,' Arthur warns. His joy fizzles into worry.

Libby reaches the first level, joining the nanny goat, which she uses as a prop to hoist herself higher.

Arthur moves closer. He glances at Kurt, who frowns. 'This is not wise,' the German says.

The wet statue proves to be a fickle handhold. Libby loses her grip, her boots scrabble for a foothold, miss. She yelps, slides inelegantly down the rock and tumbles to the wet, white earth.

Kurt reaches her first, Arthur at his heels, pulse thudding.

Libby hauls herself to a sitting position, grabs Kurt's offered hand, and tries to stand. 'Aaggh!' She plumps to the ground. Her face is white, strained with pain. Her left foot twists at an odd angle. 'Damn, damn, damn,' she cries. 'What an idiot.'

Arthur hovers. He wants to comfort her, has no idea how, or what to do.

Kurt is practical. 'We must take off the boot,' he says, kneeling to unlace the tie. 'Before the swelling makes the pain come more.' He eases the boot off, prods oh-so-gently at the already enlarged ankle.

Libby winces, gasps. Above Kurt's bent head, she clenches her teeth at Arthur. 'No dancing tonight, I guess,' she says.

Arthur hurts for her, hating this sudden transformation from exaggerated fun to pain. Thank God it seems to be no more than an ankle. He glares at the slippery nanny goat, needing something to blame for Libby's injury.

Kurt stands, digs in his coat pocket and pulls out his car keys which he throws to Arthur. 'The hotel is not far?' Arthur nods, eyes on Libby, who rocks back and forth, moaning. 'Bring the car to the bottom of the track. I meet you there, and we drive to the hospital.'

Arthur looks to Libby for permission to leave her. Her white skin is shiny with perspiration, her eyes shut tight. Kurt has one arm about her shoulders, keeping her warm.

Clutching the keys, Arthur sets off. The snow slips under his feet and he cannot run. He has to do with fast walking, glad of his thick-soled boots which he wears on construction sites. He's grateful to have this practical task to do.

As he leaves, he hears Kurt say to Libby, 'Hold on to me. I will carry you.'

And mingled with Arthur's worry is a sharp question. Why is Kurt doing the carrying? Why not himself?

Chapter Fourteen

'ARE YOU BLUSHING, DEAR?' MRS Harrington lifts her skinny nightie-clad arm to press her hand to her chin. Her thin lips curve in a teasing smile.

Maggie forces herself to return the smile. 'Hot in here,' she says.

'And Dr Elliott?' The smile broadens.

Yes. And Dr Elliott?

During Maggie, Luke and Veronica's return drive to the city in the early winter evening, Luke had chatted about the winery, the family who have run it for one hundred years, the wines, the cheese and bread provided by their host and which sufficed for lunch – in fact, anything except his ex-girlfriend.

Veronica responded brightly from the rear seat, and Maggie wished she'd offered to sit there herself, given up the front to a person willing to talk. While she grudgingly acceded that, with Veronica in the car, this was neither the time nor the place for a heart-to-heart, an apology, however short, would have soothed her frazzled temper.

After Luke dropped his sister at her flat, the silence in the car was lightened only by the regular creak of the windscreen wipers and the swish of other cars passing, sending briefly lit showers of water their way. The dense atmosphere weighed on Maggie's shoulders, as tangible as the rain spattering the glass and blurring the outside world.

Luke concentrated on the wet road. When he pulled up outside Maggie's home, she turned to face him.

'Luke–'

He reached out an arm to press a finger to her lips. 'Let me say what I need to first, please?'

Maggie tilted her head to the side in a yes motion. It wouldn't change what she knew had to be said.

'Cecily was out of order today. There was no reason for her to behave like she did.' Luke rubbed his chin. 'She doesn't mean to be cruel.'

Maggie doubted this. She didn't contradict him, however, as neither would an argument about Cecily's cruelty alter the outcome of this conversation.

'She has this killer instinct,' Luke said, 'where she needs to prey on whomever she perceives is the weakest person in the room.'

'And that was me.' Maggie was mortified over again. She's unused to being considered weak.

'The woman got it wrong this time.' Luke patted Maggie's arm. 'You're far from a shrinking violet. I knew that before I started seeing you, listening to you talking to the patients and other nurses, watching you take on us doctors when you saw we needed it.' He laughed. 'Brave of you.' A pause to allow the laughter to die, to be serious. 'You have views, opinions, Maggie. More than that, you're eager to live different experiences, learn new things.' He tapped the steering wheel, staring at her. 'They're the reasons I love being around you.'

Maggie was not appeased. Learn things. Like she was in training to be … what? A girlfriend he can be proud of? She was reminded of the play, *Pygmalion*, and how the insufferable professor bullied poor Eliza simply for the sake of passing her off as someone she wasn't. He didn't create a polished lady. He created a fake. Was Maggie right the first time, that she's Luke's Eliza Doolittle?

'Thank you,' she said, restraining her sarcasm. 'I enjoy being around you, too.'

'Good! I'm glad.' He clasped her hand. 'I'm forgiven? We can forget Cecily and her arrogance and pretend she doesn't exist? Right?'

'Wrong.' Maggie shook her head. 'The thing is, Luke, I'm not cut out for your world.' Nothing said in the last few moments had changed her mind. If anything, Luke had dug a bigger hole for himself, and Maggie's intuitive determination rested on firmer ground.

'Yes you are.' His grip tightened, as if he would convince her through sheer pressure.

Maggie gently wriggled her hand free. Luke let it go.

'Apart from your sister,' she said, 'your friends ignore me and I understand why. It's completely reasonable. I don't exist in the society they inhabit. They have nothing to talk to me about, and I have nothing to talk to them about.'

'No, no, that's not true.'

He offered no instances of how Maggie had been welcomed by his circle, or what she and they had in common. There were none.

She waited for him to understand this before twisting to open the car door. The rain had stopped. The night air smelled like freshly washed sheets, carrying the delicate scent of the pines growing through her father's wrought-iron arch above the driveway gates. Maggie breathed it in.

'Don't go yet.' Luke leaned across from the driver's seat, pushing at the door to keep Maggie from closing it.

She peered in. 'I'll see you at work,' she said. 'Please tell Veronica thank you from me, that I appreciated her friendship.' She pushed the door firmly, closing it, and walked along the gravelled path to the house, fumbling for her key by the glow of the porch light.

Mrs Harrington's eyes have narrowed, sensing Maggie's hesitation.

'Have I got it all wrong, dear,' she says. 'About you and Dr Luke?'

Maggie picks up the water jug from the bedside stand, checks the level. 'We did see each other for a while,' she says into the jug. She lifts her head and gives Mrs Harrington a smile she hopes is forgiving, kind. The old lady shouldn't be made to feel embarrassed. 'It's over. He's lovely, as you say. Just not my type.'

◇◇◇◇◇

Avoiding Luke Elliott in the hospital is impossible, despite its wandering corridors, which take more years than

The Past can Wait

Maggie has worked there to navigate confidently. She must accompany him on ward rounds when their hours coincide; she comes across him in the canteen, eating one-handed while thumbing through patients' folders; and she passes him often in those meandering corridors. He searches her out, she is sure, at the nurses' station, in the pharmacy. He doesn't talk to her, not during working hours. His eyes, however, carry an invitation to Maggie to change her mind, he is waiting.

When they do rounds together, other nurses whisper among themselves, eyes sliding to the doctor and Maggie. She naively wondered at their dedicated interest in her love life, until she realised it isn't *her* love life they care about. They want their flirty doctor returned to them, together with their own chances of capturing his heart.

With June no longer working, Maggie eats alone in the cafeteria. She's beginning to dread day shifts and is always ready to volunteer for the long nights when being by yourself is the norm. Besides, the nights give her the chance to chat quietly with Mrs Harrington, when the old lady is well enough to talk, and sleepless. Maggie learns about her children, grandchildren and the husband whom she loved and was taken from her in the first war.

'A Gallipoli casualty,' she tells Maggie. 'A long time ago.' She stares at a narrow gap between the curtains drawn around her bed. Yellow electric light, dimmed in these early hours, shows beyond the gap like a summons to a brighter day. 'We'll meet again soon. Hope he remembers me.' The old lady offers Maggie a ragged smile.

Maggie's lips quiver. Is this what it means to have found your soul mate? She closes her eyes. How long will it take Arthur to forget her? And she him? Is he already forgetting her?

Afterwards, on the dawn bus home, Maggie realises it was Arthur, no one else, whom Mrs Harrington's question conjured. She blames her tiredness after the long shift for the tears which well and need to be brushed away. If Arthur would write, or telephone … He hasn't, doesn't. Does he hold any regrets?

While Luke is discreet at work, he must have a schedule of Maggie's shifts because he calls her at home every two or three days. She leaves her mother to answer the phone, shaking her head, no, when the black handset is held out to her.

Nancy covers the mouthpiece, frowning, hissing, 'Take it.' She pushes the receiver closer, until Maggie leaves the room, hearing her mother apologising, saying she has no idea where her daughter is and she'll be sure to tell her Luke called.

'What's going on?' Nancy asks after the third call. 'A lovers' quarrel?' Her eyes manage to convey both humour and anxiety.

Maggie puts down the Australian Women's Weekly she's pretending to read and stretches her toes to the open fire. 'We never were lovers, Mum.'

'I should hope not. You know what I mean.'

'It's over. Whatever it was, it's over.' Maggie can't help herself. The need to vent her angry shame makes her spit the words. 'You can stop dreaming of a white wedding and you queening it over everyone as the mother-of-the-bride. Not gonna happen.' With Luke, or anyone. She retrieves the magazine, flips it open at random, and hides her self-pitying tears, hating herself for shedding them.

◇◇◇◇◇

Veronica's tiny flat on the first floor of a nineteenth century converted mansion in an inner suburb is highly stylish. She studied design, she once told Maggie, and these days 'tinkers with bits and pieces for friends. Home decoration a specialty.'

The furniture is all sharp angles, polished wood, steel, and brightly coloured upholstery. Bold abstract paintings fill the walls. An electric radiator casts a minimal circle of warmth in the chilly room, and Maggie wishes she could have kept her coat on.

She sits in the offered low yellow chair, which is at the edge of the warmth, and stares about while Veronica makes coffee. Leaning back, Maggie finds herself at an uncomfortable angle and shuffles forward on the seat, pulling herself upright. If she ever has her own home, she will decorate it with less style and more comfort.

'Now,' Veronica says when the coffee is poured into wide-mouthed, oversized cups sitting on too-big saucers. 'How are you, Maggie?' Her puckered forehead and pinched mouth suggest this is not a run-of-the-mill polite inquiry.

'Good.' Maggie gains a hazy insight into the motivation behind this invite, issued yesterday by telephone. If she's correct, she should drink her coffee – tasty coffee it is too, not instant – and leave. She takes another sip.

Veronica sighs gustily. 'I'm glad, though I'm not sure I believe you.' She wriggles forward to peer more closely. 'What happened at the winery was unforgiveable, and I've told my brother he needs to apologise profusely. Chocolates and roses at the least.'

There have been no chocolates or roses, for which Maggie is grateful. Returning them would be difficult. She responds to Veronica's mildly joking tone with a quick lift of her lips.

'To tell the truth,' Veronica says, 'Cecily can be, to put it plainly, a bitch. All she wanted to do was drive a wedge between you and Luke, for her own amusement.' She wrinkles her pert nose. 'She mustn't be allowed to get away with it, not this time.'

Maggie is confused. The damage to her once-robust confidence has been done. And she and Luke are no longer together. Cecily has gotten away with it. 'What do you mean?'

'Don't you see?' Veronica arches her eyebrows into a question. 'She's jealous, simple as that.' She throws out her hands. 'Too bad, is what I say.'

The urge to leave grows stronger. But Veronica is Luke's sister, and Maggie understands how sisters need to have their brothers' backs on occasion. She's had to have Teddy's back since they were kids. It never stops. Besides, Maggie likes Veronica. She will hear her out, be polite and grateful for whatever advice she will undoubtedly receive from the young woman, and afterwards forget this whole sorry interlude in her life.

'What I need to say ...' Veronica bends to Maggie, in confidante mode. 'Luke has been known in the past for not being, well, serious enough, about the women he dates.'

A memory sparks in Maggie's mind, part of the overhead conversation at the birthday party, about hoping Luke doesn't play with this one too long. If her memory is correct, Veronica was the person who said it.

'It's his way of covering up a real hurt he suffered a few years ago.' Veronica pauses for Maggie's dutiful, 'Really?'

'Yes. The sister of a school friend. Pretty, vivacious. They were the perfect pair.' Veronica steeples her fingers, eyes sorrowful. 'She threw him over for a barrister from Sydney, married him, and lives in a great big showy mansion on a cliff above the Harbour. Children too, last I heard.'

'And Luke's never recovered?' Maggie figures his mortifying rejection must be several years old, if the perpetrator has children, plural.

'We thought he'd *never* pull out of the doldrums, be a confirmed bachelor the rest of his life.' Veronica humphs. 'What a waste that would be.'

'I appreciate you telling me this, Veronica. It–'

'It's *why* I'm telling you which is important, Maggie.' She recovers her coffee, drinks, sets the cup on its saucer. 'You see, he changed when he met you.'

Maggie draws back, sceptical. 'Me?'

'Oh yes.' Enthusiasm bleeds into the phrase like red dye in water. 'I believe he's serious this time.'

The Past can Wait

'Why?' Maggie isn't to be won over so easily. 'What makes you say that?'

'Of course,' Veronica hedges in the face of Maggie's aggressive tone, 'I could be wrong.' She goes on the offensive. 'But I'm his sister, know him better than anyone, and I can tell you he's positively pining for you.'

Maggie recollects Luke's imploring eyes, the gentle voice he uses when addressing her at work, his studied politeness when he stands aside to allow her through doorways or helps draw screens around beds. He listens carefully when she describes a patient's behaviours, asks questions, takes her answers seriously.

Veronica allows her time to take in the implications of her statement. She brushes back an errant strand of hair, and says, 'Give him another chance, please, Maggie? Cecily can be ignored, and the others will come round in time, not that it's any of their business.'

Maggie bites her lip. Why should she hear him out? Would it change anything?

'Besides–' Veronica pulls out her trump card '–Mother says you're a total sweetheart and, in her words, exactly the kind of down-to-earth woman she would be thrilled to see Luke with.' She beams.

As Luke is exactly the kind of well-off, professional man Nancy would be over the moon to see her daughter with. Maggie holds this notion close.

'Please answer his calls, gorgeous one.' Veronica stands, walks to Maggie's side and lays manicured fingers on her shoulder. Squeezing gently, she murmurs, 'And if you don't answer his, will you promise to answer mine?'

Maggie glances up into eyes which, for once, hold a shy pleading. For a moment, she doesn't understand. When she does, her shock is brief.

She lifts her hand to cover Veronica's and returns her sober gaze. 'I'll always be your friend, Veronica, as you've been mine.'

Chapter Fifteen

THE CREAMY ENVELOPE IS HEAVY in Arthur's hand. He is surprised to see June's handwriting on the front. He carries the missive into the guest living room, sits on the over-cushioned sofa and opens the letter. A neatly written card invites Arthur to celebrate June's birthday at the end of July.

A scrawled note from Alf, with many exclamation marks, explains they are going all out to make this one special, given this is the last time they can party without needing to fork out for a babysitter and be home by midnight. *The gang will be there! We miss you, pretty much forgotten what your handsome mug looks like, ha ha. Please, please come!*

The gang includes Maggie. Arthur's pulse quickens. He rests the invitation and note on his knee and thinks about the last party Alf and June threw. A fleeting seven months ago. A lot has happened in that time. Although, to be honest, most of what's happened has been very recent. Arthur's mind is at rest over the decision he's made. His nagging disquiet has been banished.

He will accept the invitation, of course, with pleasure. And he'll tell Alf he has his own news. A surprise.

The telephone in the hall trills as Arthur passes it on his way to his room to fetch pen and paper.

'Hello,' he says into the receiver. 'Adaminaby 238, Arthur Kaine speaking.'

Libby's exuberant giggle reverberates in his ear. 'You're so formal, Arthur.' She pauses to catch her breath and giggles anew. 'You'd make a great receptionist. If you could find a company willing to trust the role to a man.'

'Ha ha ha,' Arthur mocks in return. 'Were you after me?'

'Only if there are no other good-looking men at home.' Libby is incorrigible. And fun.

'All out of them, I'm afraid,' Arthur says. 'You'll have to make do with me.'

'Ha ha, and now I'm being serious.' Libby amends her

The Past can Wait

voice to the right level of solemnity. 'Checking you're set for the weekend at the farm. Mum's in such a flurry of over-excitement I'm worried she'll have a heart attack. She keeps nagging me about this, that and the other.'

'I can understand.' Arthur pictures the motherly Mrs Walters and her need to make sure all is exactly as it should be. 'She hasn't had much time to get sorted, has she, poor woman?'

'Probably for the best. If there'd been months, she would've been a pain to be near for that much longer.' Fondness transforms Libby's words into a loving caress. 'Now, you,' she says, business-like. 'Suit organised?'

'Yep.'

'Ring?'

'Yep.'

'Car?'

'Yes, Libby. Yes, to everything. Done, including … well, you're not supposed to worry about that part.' Arthur adopts the same serious tone. 'I understand what this means to you, and I won't let you down. It'll be perfect.'

'Thank you.' Arthur hears the catch in her voice. 'Thank you. You're wonderful, you know that?'

'Wish more people would agree.' He laughs, and Libby laughs too, and there's a flurry of goodbyes and she hangs up.

Arthur stands with the buzzing receiver in his hand, staring unseeingly at Mrs Carter's print of an Albert Namatjira landscape. His parents have the same one, with the ghost gums, the arid landscape and rocky escarpment. His mother loves the painting. She says she's unlikely to ever see this area of Australia, and it makes her feel good to know there is a beautiful emptiness at the heart of the country, unspoiled by evil.

Good things, wonderful, life-changing things, Arthur whispers to himself, can happen when you least expect them. Life can be kind as well as cruel.

Libby replaces the receiver in the cradle and twirls her way into her bedroom. Happiness sparkles in her chest, a champagne-fizzing heady delirium of joy. Who knew one could feel such emotions?

She stands in front of the old wardrobe, gazing for the hundredth time at the dress falling in a waterfall of white satin and lace from its padded hanger. In their boxes on the chest of drawers, new silk knickers, bra and a camisole, rest in tissue paper. White satin shoes, a frivolous expense given the mud at the farm, sit neatly below the dress.

'Get married here, at home? This time of year?' Libby's mother waved towards the kitchen window. Low, dark clouds threatened snow. 'Is there something you need to tell me?'

A delicious heat drenched Libby's cheeks, and more of her than her face. 'No, Mother. Honestly!'

'Then why the rush?'

'It'd be better to wait for spring, I agree,' Libby countered, 'except you and Dad might not be living here, and if you are, you'll be in the throes of packing and sorting.'

'Good point,' her mother conceded. 'What about one of the nicer hotels in Cooma? I bet none of them are booked up in the winter, they'll have dates available. Easier for the guests too.'

Libby turned mulish. 'Adaminaby is my home, Mum. I want to be married in the church, before they move it.' Mulish softened into wistful. 'It's right for me to celebrate the end of my single life here, where I grew up and a place I love.'

'Sentimental nonsense,' her mother declared, sniffing tears. She laid a work-hardened hand on Libby's arm and sighed. 'Then here is where this event will take place.' She grinned. 'Your dad'll be thrilled to his back teeth, of course. Men don't understand the practicalities.'

Her mother has given her the family heirloom necklace

with its sparkling emerald to wear, the one she wore at her own wedding.

'Something old,' she told Libby when she handed the jewel over in its scuffed long box with faded lining.

'Not to borrow, Mum? Don't you want to keep it?'

Her mother shrugged. 'I've worn it maybe six times. It'll suit you a lot better, love, with your red hair.'

'Auburn.'

'Yes, of course.' Her mother pressed her lips together, eyes teasing. 'Auburn.'

Libby purchased the dress with her own money. She expected to have to go to Sydney to find her vision, but there it was, in Cooma's one bridal shop, waiting for her. A sign.

The stars had aligned.

Libby remembers a conversation with June, when her friend suggested finding someone who would take her seriously would be hard, because Libby was never serious about men, with her flirtatious eyes and pretend coyness.

Libby had batted her eyelids in self-mockery. 'I'll know the right man when he comes along,' she told June. 'And I'll be my real self for him.'

And the right man has come along, and she is her real self for him.

Chapter Sixteen

'THESE ARE A GOOD IDEA.' Maggie holds out a carton of paper plates for June's inspection. 'No washing up, no need to ask your friends to bring their spare crockery.'

'You sound like an advertisement.' June stretches over her pregnant belly to read the label. She gives Maggie a wry glance. 'We could put you on the wireless, convince the listening public what a good idea paper plates are.'

Maggie bridles at the perceived mockery, before laughing. Her moods are volatile these days, and down far more than up. The most innocent of comments can get her gander up, and when that includes a joke from the kind and gentle June, Maggie understands what a bad way she's in. She was doing well, getting there – wherever there is – until she stupidly agreed to see Veronica. The conversation with Luke's sister slithers around her brain, contradictory fragments hard to catch and hold tight.

Luke not serious about the women he dates ... never got over it ... changed when he met you ...

Luke hasn't called since, which means Maggie hasn't had to decide whether she will talk to him or not. Her mother's daily Gestapo-like interrogations drive Maggie crazy.

'Why hasn't your doctor rung recently?' she said yesterday, with an accusing frown. 'You see him at the hospital, don't you? Been talking there, right? Still seeing him, aren't you?'

Maggie, cosy in front of the fire with a new Georgette Heyer, snapped. She shouted. 'How many times do I have to tell you, Mum? It's over, finished, done with.'

Nancy reeled back with the drama of a silent movies' star, pressing a fluttering hand to her bosom.

'Just watching out for my one and only daughter, if you don't bloomin' mind?' She stalked to the kitchen where her loud complaints to Maggie's ever-patient dad flowed freely into the living room.

Maggie should be done with men. She should explore

The Past can Wait

Veronica's silent invitation. The tempting vision of her mother's horror makes her grin.

Cheered, Maggie returns to the paper plates. 'We buy these?' she says, all party business. 'And the serviettes?'

'Sure.' June takes the box and walks to the Woolworths' counter to pay for the basket of goodies she and Maggie have accumulated.

Maggie waits with her in the queue, her mind roving to the last party at June's house. Nearly seven months, the longest she and Arthur have been apart since they met in the migrant camp in 1949.

The camp was fun, life simple, if you didn't mind living in a Nissen hut. She smiles at the memories – of being Teddy's go-between when he courted Raine; of Raine's birthday treat at Luna Park where Alf tried, with useless bravery, to stop his blushes whenever Raine spoke to him; and Teddy's 21st birthday party. Her smile falters.

The party was when her heart first stirred for Arthur, the look they shared when Teddy was doing one of his rants, this time about the Snowy Mountains Scheme which had been launched the same day. Ironic that a party and the Scheme should be both the beginning and the end for her and Arthur.

The end. Her stomach quivers. Damn the man. Maggie misses him as badly as she did months ago. Has she been foolish, selfish? The mountains are hardly the Black Hole of Calcutta. Would it have hurt her so much to leave her life here for a time, to be with the man she supposedly loves?

On occasion, in an expansive mood, Arthur talked about the magnificence of the country there – of undulating plains and soaring peaks, of greenery and snow, and the vastness of the star-washed sky. Maggie would tease, saying those mountains meant more to him than she did, not meaning it because it wasn't true. And Arthur would assure her, no, never, and hold her and kiss her into content agreement.

He'd urged her to visit, more than once. Maggie refused,

believing the mountains were a temporary glitch in her and Arthur's road to settled happiness, and why should she drag herself all that way?

What would happen if she invited herself there now, turned up unannounced? The idea sits uncomfortably in her chest.

'Come on.' June has paid. She hands Maggie two bags, keeps two for herself. 'Let's go. My legs are about to give way and if I don't have a cup of tea soon, I'll collapse.'

June's face is pinched, pale. Maggie eases the two remaining bags from her friend's grasp and leads the way to the bus stop. June's Volkswagen is in the repair shop with a dent to its rear wheel arch – not June's fault, she tells everyone. June is no hurry to retrieve it, reluctant to drive with her stomach pushed into the steering wheel.

At the house, Maggie lights the kerosene heater to ward the chill from the room, and insists June sits comfortably in the living room while she makes the tea. She finds biscuits in a cupboard, puts them on a plate, and carries a tray bearing teapot, cups and biscuits into the room. June's cheeks are touched with pink from the heater's warmth, and she is deeply engrossed in the letter she pulled from the letterbox by the gate as they arrived.

'Good news?' Maggie sets the tray on the low table.

June startles and lays the single page, face down, on the couch beside her. 'From my friend, Libby.' Her voice is strained.

'Libby? Oh yes, another one of us nurses.' Maggie sits on a stool by the table, pours the tea and nudges the cup close to June. 'What does she have to say?' She grimaces. 'Not that it's any of my business.' She begins to pour tea for herself.

'Maggie.'

June's tone causes Maggie to set the teapot on the table. For some reason, her hands shake. Libby is from up there, the mountains, where Arthur is. Her imagination flies to

The Past can Wait

Teddy's accident. Her brother nearly died in a losing battle with a frontloader careening down a snowy slope into the land rover he was a passenger in.

'Is it Arthur?' Her voice trembles. 'Has there been an accident?'

'An accident?' June frowns. 'No, no, nothing like that.' She rests a hand on her belly. 'Sorry, Mags, I didn't mean to frighten you.'

'Then what?'

June picks up the letter. She handles the one page scrawl with the same care Maggie has seen her deal with a newborn baby. 'Typical Libby, short, lacking necessary detail …' She squints at the writing as if the necessary detail will come to light on a second reading, and sighs.

'What in hell?' Stress raises the pitch of Maggie's voice. 'If it's to do with me, it must be about Arthur. For God's sake, tell me.' She itches to tear the page from June's fluttering fingers.

'Libby says …' June reads the barely legible writing. *'June, dear June, I hope you will be thrilled for me, because I was remembering what you said once about how I had to be the real me to find a man to love me for myself …'*

Maggie is confused. She opens her mouth to ask what Libby's love life has to do with her. And shuts it as realisation crashes her chest with the force of the bombs she left behind.

June reads on – *'… and I have, June!! I have. He loves me for me, with all my quirks, and this is IT, different from anything else, from anyone else, and by the time you receive this, I'll be a married woman!! Wish me well. I'm the LUCKIEST girl in the world!!'*

Nausea rises up Maggie's gorge. Don't let it be what's hurtling around her head. Don't let it be the notion which grips her stomach like a vice, tearing at her gut. She forces the words from her mouth.

'Does she mean Arthur?' She holds her breath.

June stares at her. 'Libby doesn't say, but, Maggie … I'm

119

sorry, it has to be Arthur.'

'Why?' Maggie's confusion rises, swirls with the emotional waves battering her heart.

'Libby bumped into Arthur, in Cooma, when he went back after New Year.' June gabbles, getting it all out. 'He helped her family with some Authority business, and they became friendly–'

'Friendly!' Maggie shoves the stool out from under her, stands over June. 'You knew your mate was seeing Arthur, that they were friendly, and you didn't bother to mention this to me? To Arthur's ex-fiancée, and your supposed best friend?' Fury snakes its venomous way into her words. 'Well, best friend apart from the better best friend you connive with behind my back.'

'No,' June wails. She presses into the sofa cushions, clasps protective arms around her stomach. 'You told me it was over between you and Arthur. You said you were happy with Luke.'

'And then I wasn't.' Maggie whirls away, strides to the window. She stands with her back to the golden lit scene of evening sunshine, grass, and young trees. Her hurt, her anger, stifle mere tears. 'Didn't you notice?' she shouts. 'Didn't me telling you it was over with the gorgeous doctor make you suspect it was *over*?'

June stands too, holding her side. Maggie winces, won't let her righteous fury falter.

'Maggie, listen, please.' June takes a step forward, hands outstretched. 'I've heard nothing from Libby for months. If I thought about it, which I didn't, I assumed she'd moved on. That's what she's like, a gadfly where men are concerned. Loses her heart to one and the next week to another.'

'Assumed?'

June carries on. 'And as for you and Luke.' She throws up her hands. 'Can't you see? He loves you, he's perfect for you. You can't mope for Arthur for the rest of your life–'

'I can't now, can I?'

The Past can Wait

June takes another tentative step. '–and Luke is here, waiting for you.'

Maggie steps around her traitorous friend. 'If I stay, I'll say things which can't be unsaid.' She walks swiftly into the hall, takes her coat from the wooden stand, and lets herself out of the house.

The tears come as she strides in the freezing dusk to the bus stop, struggling to push her arms into the coat sleeves, to do up buttons while battling the blustery wind. There are tears at June's betrayal. More than that, her tears are hot and bitter at Arthur's too soon readiness to love again.

Again? Did he ever love her?

Maggie's sobs won't be stifled. She walks past the stop, keeps going, past another. Five stops later, her tears are exhausted. A bus pulls in as she nears the shelter. Ignoring the curious, occasionally sympathetic glances of her fellow passengers, Maggie touches her forehead to the cold bus window and closes her heavy-lidded eyes, as if darkness will soothe her. Her chest thumps, with the walk and with the whirl of emotion which refuses to calm.

When she reaches home, no lights welcome her, and her father's car is absent from the drive. Maggie lets herself in, whooshing a soft sigh of relief at being alone. In the kitchen, she pours a glass from the tap, leans against the sink and gulps the water. A note on the table from Nancy says they are visiting Teddy, Raine and the kids, and last night's stew is in the fridge for Maggie to re-heat. Maggie dry heaves at the idea of food, despite not having eaten since breakfast. She had rushed from her shift to meet June, to help her friend out.

Maggie snorts.

June. Later, when she has sorted her feelings about Arthur and Libby, Maggie will think more about June. For now, there's a placeholder, like a bookmark, at the point where she questions the truth of their friendship. They have known each other for less than a year. Not time enough to understand where another person's loyalties lie. Apparently.

Arthur is the true heartbreak. Maggie's wonderings whether he was missing her, why didn't he ring or write – all make sense. He wasn't missing her. He didn't ring or write because he didn't care. Another woman consoled him, if he needed consoling.

She rinses the glass, sets it on the draining board above the pink kitchen cupboard and walks with leaden feet to her bedroom.

Sleep refuses to relieve her of her misery. The wind buffets the window, and an icy draught fingers the edges of the blind, sending it quivering before exploring further into the room. Maggie curls in her bed, pressing her cheek into the pillow, and picks over the argument which started the whole trouble.

She examines the thought she had in the Woolworth's queue, about how she'd been too ready to reject Arthur's enthusiastic compromise. She sees his face lit up with delight, believing he'd found a solution which let them be together without him sacrificing his dream to own their home. It's true she has no wish to live in the back of beyond, especially in a town which will soon be under water. It doesn't change the fact that if she and Arthur were truly committed to each other, they could have found a way, like sensible adults. Losing her temper, storming out, breaking off the engagement …

The front door closes with a click, the light from the passage shines under Maggie's door, her mother whispers, and her father grunts a response. Her parents, married for over thirty years, who have survived a war together, migrated to the other side of the world and found a new life, together. Maggie rolls over. The bed springs creak their familiar complaint.

She could have spent time in the mountains, for Arthur, for her love for him. Hell, she might have liked it. No chance to find out. Not now. He's lost to her, and she's to

The Past can Wait

blame. Maggie buries her head in her pillow. She failed the test of love before she was even committed.

Is she about to do the same with Luke Elliott? Is the treacherous June right, that Luke loves her? What chance has she given herself of returning that love, moping instead for a man she can never have?

Sleep finds her at last, brief and restless. When the alarm jangles her into wakefulness, Maggie showers, dresses in her uniform and goes to the kitchen to make tea. While she waits for the kettle to boil, she walks into the living room to the telephone. Veronica's number is scribbled on the pad, where Nancy jotted it down for Maggie to call. It's five in the morning, but Maggie's determination might not last to a civilised hour.

'Yes? Is there an emergency?' Veronica is querulous and fearful.

'No, no,' Maggie says. 'It's Maggie Greene here.'

'Maggie? What–'

'The conversation we had. Tell Luke, yes, I'll answer his call.' She hangs up, and it's not until she is pushing open the doors to the Royal's entrance that she realises she didn't apologise for the ungodly hour of her call.

Cheryl Burman

Chapter Seventeen

ARTHUR'S JOURNEY HOME TO THE city is long, and not without its troubling thoughts. The decisions he's made have lifted his spirits. He's at ease in that respect, more than he has been for a long time, he can now admit. It was time to let go.

But now the future stretches along a different road than the one he had expected, he's deeply unsettled to be returning to the old familiarities.

He dozes on the night train from Melbourne, disturbed by the snuffles and shiftings of his fellow passengers trying to rest their bodies in the upright seats. A sleeper would have been quieter. It would also be a waste of money. Horizontal, or sitting, Arthur could not have slept.

Maggie is uppermost in his thoughts. How will she greet his news? Or will she be so wrapped up in her new man she won't give a fig for Arthur's great surprise? He wriggles in the seat, crosses and uncrosses his legs, and waits for dawn to shed light on the landscape. Daylight brings a shrouding mist as opaque as the night.

Arriving at last, Arthur hauls his cardboard case from the rack and waits for the line of dishevelled, grumpy people to disembark. He will go home first, as he promised his parents, eat and try to sleep. A clear head is needed for his visit to Alf and June this evening, when he will find out firsthand how things are with Maggie. And the doctor. Time and facts will prepare him for seeing her at June's party. Seeing her – and him.

◇◇◇◇◇

'Arthur!' Alf opens the door, peers behind Arthur like he's expecting another visitor. He briefly shakes his head at the stubborn emptiness and steps aside to let his guest into the hall.

'Come on in,' he says, leading the way to the living room.

The Past can Wait

'Got the heater going in here, full blast. Freezing weather, not what we migrated ten thousand miles for, hey?'

The disquiet Arthur carried all the way from Adaminaby rises again at Alf's tone with its forced cheeriness, undoing the good the conversation with his parents had done.

'It's the right decision,' his father said. 'As long as you're happy.'

'A sudden one,' his mother said, eyebrows arched. 'But I agree with your dad, and can't wait to–'

What she can't wait for was cut off by the phone sending a summons loudly through the house. Arthur could guess, however.

In Alf's warmish living room, ushered to a seat near the kerosene heater, Arthur worries he shouldn't have come here after all.

'Beer?'

'Thanks, yeah.'

Alf leaves, returns with two bottles of Coopers lager and tall glasses. 'June'll kill me if she finds us drinking from the bottle.' He laughs, keeping the strained tone, and sets the glasses on coasters on the low table.

'Where is she?' Arthur keeps his own voice casual, doesn't want to ask what's going on, although it's clear as the cold sun outside that something is. 'She's not still working, is she?'

'Nah.' Alf carefully pours the frothing liquid and hands the glass to Arthur. 'Though she *is* at the Royal, visiting a friend who had to go in for a minor op.' He winks. 'Women's stuff. I didn't ask.'

'Good move.' Arthur relaxes. This is the banter he's used to from Alf. He shouldn't be so sensitive.

Alf plumps onto the two-seater sofa and raises his glass. 'To new beginnings,' he says, and moves straight on without pausing for a response. 'And I have to confess to being hurt you didn't tell me about your new beginning.'

Arthur raises his glass automatically, brow furrowed.

Why should Alf be hurt? He's planning on telling him today, had said in his letter accepting the party invite he had news and he wanted it to be a surprise.

'Sorry. I thought it best to tell you in person,' he says. 'Wanted to see the expression on your face.' He grins. 'Should I wait 'til June's here? Make you hang on, break it all at once?'

Alf doesn't return the grin. 'June knows. In fact, she told me. Which is why I'm annoyed, hearing big news in a roundabout fashion about one of my oldest and closest mates – remember, we met on the ship coming out–'

'June knows?'

'–and,' Alf rants on, 'this old china plate can't be bothered letting me know he's getting hitched.' He shakes his head. 'Let alone have the decency to ask me to be his best man. Me or Teddy.'

'Hitched? Married?' Arthur slowly returns his glass to the table, shifts it to the coaster before its damp bottom can vandalise the varnished wood.

'Hitched, as in wedded, like me and June did last year.' Alf peers at Arthur, frowning. 'Like you and Libby did a short time ago.'

Arthur stares. How on earth …?

'I'm on top of the world thrilled for you, if that's what you want, and for Libby.' Alf waves the beer, the rant waning. 'She's a sweet woman under the frivolous flirting. She deserves a decent fellow like you, Arthur–'

'Libby? Married?' Arthur finally gets it, although he's no idea where this comes from. 'No, no!' He holds up his hands, palms out. 'Not me and Libby! That's not my surprise news. Mine's not near as dramatic.' He takes a breath. 'Mine's only to say I've resigned from the Authority and I'm coming home for good. That's it, no more!'

'Resigned? Home for good?' Alf appears to have trouble grasping the words.

Arthur helps his old friend out. 'I love the mountains,

The Past can Wait

they've grown on me. You saw for yourself how magnificent the land is up there.' He rests his palms on his knees, going over for the umpteenth time the thoughts which have led him here. 'I did what I set out to do, got cash together for a house.' He grunts. 'If it was worth it.' And moves on quickly before he travels too far down that road. 'And then I got to thinking how I didn't have a life up there, after nearly six years. You, June, Teddy – all of you are here, getting on with things.' He gives Alf an arch look. 'Having babies. I don't want to miss out any more. I want to be part of it all.'

And I want to see if I have any chance still with Maggie, he doesn't add out loud. He hasn't yet discovered the lay of the land there.

'Kind of like the Prodigal Son?' Alf shakes himself out of his shock.

'I guess so.' Arthur nods. 'As for where you and June got this notion about me marrying Libby …' Laughter catches in his throat. Libby told him she'd written to June, broken the good news about the wedding. Seems she left out the most important bit, like who she was marrying.

Alf stares. 'Great that you're back, welcome home, honest it's wonderful news. But I gotta ask, what the hell's all this about Libby and the man of her dreams being you?'

Arthur lets the laugh escape. 'Not a clue, mate. All I can tell you is that Libby married a work colleague of mine, a German friend, our finance man.' He grins. 'I introduced them, and love blossomed when Libby fell off that goat statue in Cooma, the one up on the lookout. Broke her ankle, and Kurt – that's the German – carried her to the hospital.'

'A German?' Alf winces.

'One of the good guys,' Arthur says. 'One day I'll tell you.' He picks up his beer, takes a swallow. 'Kurt and Libby are madly in love, were married two weeks ago on her mum and dad's station. Bloody freezing it was, but she insisted.' He recaptures the joy of the day – Kurt's face-splitting grins, Libby's eyes full of love, her brother Rob's initial wariness melting at the bliss his sister radiated. And Mr and Mrs Walters happily dazed, welcoming everyone, being perfect hosts.

'I was Kurt's best man, in fact,' he says, 'and, Alf, if I ever get married, you'll be mine. Not Teddy, too unreliable.' He's relieved to have the source of the tension sorted. Silly misunderstandings. Always best to talk, face to face.

Alf sits straight on the sofa. 'Thanks,' he says. His voice is flat as he takes time to digest this new truth. He gulps his beer, waves the half-empty glass. 'We thought, me and June, you didn't tell us because of Maggie, that you were embarrassed, upset. I've no idea what, something anyway, and you didn't want us to know, not yet.'

Maggie. Her name, spoken out loud, jolts Arthur into a sickening realisation. Nausea builds in the pit of his stomach, killing the remnants of his humour over the French farce of a mix up.

'Does Maggie think I'm married?'

'Yeah, mate, she does.' Alf's eyes slide sideways and Arthur's nausea roils.

'And what does she think about it?' He drags the reluctant question from his throat.

Alf draws in a breath. 'She wasn't thrilled.'

Arthur's chest loosens. There's a chance he might, possibly, with luck and tact, be able to put everything right. Before he can ask the question he desperately wants to – and is as desperately afraid of knowing the answer to – the question about how serious Maggie is about this doctor, Alf carries on.

'Think she's all right these days.' Alf won't meet Arthur's eyes. 'Seems set up with Luke, the handsome, rich doctor. According to June, Dr Luke is head-over-heels in love with our Mags, keen as mustard.' Alf fidgets with his glass, sets it down, and rests his hands on his knees. His fingers are of great interest to him.

The Past can Wait

The silence hangs as heavy as this morning's mist outside the train window, and as cold.

'That's it, then.' Arthur stares past Alf to the wall, wanting to disappear into the muted grey and yellow rectangles of the very modern wallpaper. 'What I expected.' Despite expecting it, he's devastated, as broken as he was seven months ago. 'No more than I deserve after … after everything.'

Making her wait, the nonsense about asking her to come to the mountains. He shifts his gaze to Alf, searching for and finding sympathy. 'I've been a bloody fool, haven't I?'

'I'm sorry,' Alf says. 'Really sorry.'

◇◇◇◇◇

Maggie has insisted Luke not fetch her in his car this evening. The car is too intimate. She wants to meet him at the restaurant, test her feelings, test his reactions to seeing her, in a neutral atmosphere.

He wasn't working the day Maggie rang Veronica, which meant she sidestepped any awkward moment of whether he knew of the call or not. Veronica didn't delay in passing on the message, however. Maggie hadn't been home half an hour when the phone rang.

Nancy answered, and from the kitchen Maggie heard her dour 'Yes, she's here. I can see if–' Silence. 'That right?' Her voice trilled with joy. 'Good news, Luke, good news. I'll fetch her.'

Maggie sat with her arms folded on the table, not moving until she was summoned.

'Mags, it's Luke,' Nancy whispered hoarsely. 'Again.' Jabbing a finger in the direction of the living room and the telephone, she kept the whisper going. 'He says you'll talk to him this time.' She squinted at Maggie. 'You will, won't you? Poor man, he's been horribly patient.'

Standing, Maggie ignored her mother's praise of the rejected suitor and walked, steadily, no haste, to the phone. She picked up the handpiece. 'Maggie here.'

'Thank God, Maggie. I wasn't sure you'd come to the phone. It's great to hear your voice.'

He'd heard it the previous day when they both attended the fast fading Mrs Harrington. Maggie let it go.

'I told Veronica I'd listen. What do you want to say, Luke?'

'A lot.' He laughed, grew instantly serious. 'Let me take you to dinner tomorrow night. You don't have to work, I checked. I want to sort things out between us.'

In the pause, Maggie's thoughts carried themselves of their own volition to Arthur. Had he wanted to sort things out between them? If he had, her own obstinacy had gotten in the way, until the reality of his marriage jolted her into a cruel understanding. Unlike Luke, Maggie would never have the chance to sort anything out between her and Arthur. She should give Luke a chance. After all, as June said, he was here, waiting for her. What was there to lose?

'It would be nice to have dinner with you.' Her level tone didn't quell his enthusiasm.

'Fantastic, that's great. I'll pick you up at seven, take you somewhere special, a real treat. You'll love it.'

'No.'

'No?' His voice faltered. 'You don't want to go?'

'I mean no, don't pick me up. Tell me where and when, and I'll meet you there.'

'But—'

'Please, Luke. I find my own way, or I don't come.'

He huffed loudly into the phone. 'Fine.' The words verged on snappish. 'I'm driving you home afterwards, no argument.'

That was the deal they struck, and now Maggie sits on the bus, her winter coat pulled close over a black pencil skirt topped with a red angora twinset dressed with pearl buttons. Nancy had been thrilled to be asked to comb Maggie's hair into a French knot, and had loaned her a colourful light scarf to finish the outfit off.

The Past can Wait

'Losing that bit of weight suits you, Mags.' Nancy eyed her critically, brushed a tiny piece of white lint from the short cardigan. 'He's a lucky man, this doctor.' She smiled widely, showing nicotine-stained teeth. 'You'll make a beautiful bride … when the time comes,' she added at Maggie's glare. 'We'll do it properly this time,' Nancy muttered, helping Maggie into her coat. 'Not like that horrid rushed affair of your brother's.'

She stood back for a final inspection, nodded, and leaned in to kiss Maggie lightly on the cheek, an unusual gesture. Despite the close smell of cigarettes, Maggie was grateful. She needed courage tonight. It was why she had chosen to take care with her dress, her hair and makeup. She wanted to feel confident. To believe she could be comfortable, at ease, in Luke's world.

The bus pulls into the stop and Maggie moves to the front. The frosty air on her face when she steps onto the pavement reminds her of London winters, trying to tempt warmth from a meagre coal fire. Life has changed in many ways since those days, and for the better. Is it time for more change, to put that past further behind her?

Maggie hugs her handbag close and steps towards the restaurant. The answer to her own question hangs in the balance. She will see what happens tonight.

Chapter Eighteen

ARTHUR HAS NO WISH TO break the silence in the living room with the modern wallpaper. He wants to sit there, listening to the hiss of the kerosene heater, letting the world go on without him. The click of the front door forces him to face life.

Alf jumps to his feet and walks into the hallway. 'June! You're home. Are you freezing? Tea?'

'Tea would be lovely, thanks. You're a darling as ever.' Tiredness leaks into June's words.

'How's your friend?'

'Good, the op went well. But I learned something today, Alf.' Distress adds to the tiredness. 'I have to tell Maggie, and when I do, she'll hate me even more.'

There are shuffling sounds, as of a coat being removed, and Alf says, too brightly, 'You'll never guess who's here.'

In the murmured silence, Arthur hauls himself from the chair and takes the three steps to the living room door. As he reaches it, June whispers, 'Only Arthur? No Libby?'

'Only me.'

June startles, whirls about as swiftly as she can in her ponderous state. She touches her fingers to her mouth.

'Only me,' Arthur says again. He keeps his expression neutral. 'Libby's enjoying her honeymoon in Sydney with her new husband, Kurt.' He emphasises *Kurt*, and presses his lips together. He wants to ask what June needs to tell Maggie and why Maggie will hate her more.

June glances from Arthur to Alf, and to Arthur. 'You didn't marry Libby?'

'No.'

'Who on earth is Kurt?' June narrows her eyes. 'Sounds German. Is Libby okay?'

'Oh yes.' Arthur forces his mind to stay a moment longer with Libby. 'Blissful. All good, June, all very, very good.'

June opens her mouth but Alf gently urges her forward.

The Past can Wait

'Go on in, it's warm in there. I'll make tea. Another beer?' he offers Arthur.

'Thanks.'

Arthur returns to his chair. June follows, her forehead knotted. She falls onto the sofa where Alf had been sitting, and chews her lip. Arthur hasn't seen her since early March, and in that time her face has grown rounder, her body too.

'Congratulations on the baby.' He tips his head towards June's stomach. 'Motherhood suits you. Blooming, as they say, if it's okay to compliment another man's wife.'

'I'll take the compliments wherever I can find them these days.' June wriggles in the seat, relaxes into a comfortable position. 'What's going on, Arthur? I honestly thought …'

Arthur shrugs. 'Seems when Libby told you about getting married, she forgot to say who to.' He frowns. 'One day I'll quiz you and Alf on why on earth you believed it was me.' He rubbed his chin, smoothed today of the stubble he'd allowed to grow since being clean-shaven for the wedding. 'Come to think of it, I could probably do without knowing.'

He doesn't need them to tell him, of course. The kisses on the cheek, the passing on of how much her parents liked him, the invite to the big celebration in Cooma. Arthur wasn't clueless. To be honest, given Maggie was gone from his life, he might have colluded in the pretense of romance, followed where it led, if anywhere.

Had it not been for the broken ankle.

Libby attended her parents' party with her foot in plaster, fussed over by an attentive Kurt bringing her cushions, drinks and tasty morsels of food. Arthur joked to Mrs Walters that Kurt must think Libby was Queen Elizabeth come to visit. Mrs Walters' eyebrows came together, and she paid closer attention to her daughter. An amused Arthur had to find others to talk to. Kurt and Libby had no interest in conversation with anyone outside themselves.

The friendship between the three of them is Arthur's one regret at leaving. On the other hand, he doesn't want to be the spare wheel. He has enough of that here in the city.

'So he'll be kind to her?' June isn't convinced.

'He's a great guy, June, really.' Arthur stares into her anxious eyes. 'Wasn't just ordinary people on our side suffered in that bloody war.'

June nods, slowly. 'Then I'm pleased for her.'

Right now, Arthur doesn't want to talk about Libby. Libby is the happy news. He wants to go back to June's worry for Maggie. Whatever's happened unsettles him. He needs to know.

'It's not my business, not any more,' he says, 'but can I ask why you have to ring Mags?'

Alf returns with the beer, and a cup of tea. He gives the beer to Arthur, places the tea on the table by June, and sits beside her.

'June, sweetheart, what's happened?'

June briefly closes her eyes. 'My fault, all of it. Maggie hates me and she has every reason to.' She peers at Arthur. 'Especially given you're not married.' She brings her cup close to her mouth and appraises Arthur over the rim. 'Do you love her?'

Love Maggie? Of course he loves her. He never stopped. The breakup wasn't his idea. He's moped and grieved for seven months. What's June saying?

'Whether I love Maggie or not isn't the question.' He sets the bottle of beer on its coaster. 'She's happy with her fancy doctor, right? What can I offer her? At this moment, I'm jobless and living with my parents. A great catch.'

'Jobless?'

'I'll explain later, love.' Alf strokes June's arm. 'Tell us what's going on.'

'I will. First, I have to tell you, Arthur, what you can offer Maggie.' June puts down the cup without drinking. 'A faithful, non-devious heart, that's what.' She huffs. 'I feel horrible for encouraging it.' Tears well in her eyes, and Alf puts his arm around her shoulder.

The Past can Wait

'Let it out, sweetheart. Tell us.'

Arthur clenches his fingers. Yes, for God's sake, tell us, he wants to shout.

'After I saw my friend, I wandered to the nurses' room, see who was there to say hello to. Good chat, catching up. Until I'm about to go, and Enid pulls me aside.' June sighs. 'Enid isn't popular with the other girls, too much of what's best for Enid is best for everyone. She was upset.'

Arthur waits for the meandering tale to become relevant to Maggie. June's tone, her reluctance to spill what she's heard, shadows his mind like a cartoon phantom. There is danger here.

'Enid went out for a time with Luke, about a year ago.' June twists her fingers in her lap. 'She was introduced to his friends, dinners, theatre, all the treatment. Wedding bells rang in her ears, ecstatic.' Her voice drops to a whisper, rough with possible tears. 'Until another nurse took her aside one day, whispered she shouldn't get in too deep, our doctor had done this before.' She looks directly at Arthur. 'And he'd walked away. More than once.'

Arthur's fists clench.

'Enid didn't want to hear it.' June's voice is emotionless. They all know how this ended. 'A month later, he takes her out for an expensive meal, waits for the dessert course and sweetly tells her the romance is over.'

The cartoon phantom unfurls black wings.

'Enid didn't say anything because Maggie would see it as sour grapes. Besides, Dr Elliott might be serious this time …' June stares at Arthur with wet eyes. 'He treats her well, the perfect gentleman. And he chased her hard when she was reluctant.'

She was reluctant? Arthur finds a crumb of comfort.

'When the romance seemed off, Enid forgot about it.' June clasps her arms around her stomach and rocks gently in Alf's hold. 'Yesterday, she overhead Luke on the phone at the nurses' station, calling a restaurant for a reservation for two, explaining it was for a special occasion, and could he have a table which was private.' June ceases her rocking, unclasps her arms and resumes her stare at Arthur. 'He saw Enid listening, and winked.'

Arthur digests this tale. 'A private table so he can dump her without embarrassing himself?'

'Or a private table so he can propose?' Alf offers.

Not a consoling thought, either.

'The wink was what set Enid off. Like it was a great joke. She knew it had to be Maggie, there'd been no one else since.' Tears streak June's cheeks. 'I am such, such an idiot.' She wriggles off the sofa, stands. 'Which is why I have to ring Maggie, immediately, apologise, and warn her.'

◇◇◇◇◇

The restaurant boasts a maître d' standing at a polished wooden lectern. He checks the booking, clouding his faint outrage at a woman turning up alone with a supercilious arch of his eyebrows. Maggie has timed herself to be ten minutes late, to ensure she doesn't arrive first.

The maître d' is breezily apologetic. The doctor has not yet arrived and would Mademoiselle wish to be seated at the table, or perhaps the bar where she could enjoy a drink while she waits?

Maggie chooses the table. She won't sit alone at a bar, no matter how exclusive the restaurant and, presumably, its clientele.

She hands her coat to a girl dressed in black, and is led by a summoned waiter into a golden lit, richly carpeted room, past white-linen draped tables where clean-shaven, Brylcreemed men pay close attention to red-lipsticked, coiffured women in gorgeous gowns. The sounds are of murmured talk, the clink of ice in glass and muted laughter.

Maggie resists the urge to tug at her angora twinset and touch her hair. She is underdressed. Embarrassment mixes with anger. Luke should have warned her.

Seated at a table in a corner, serviette unfolded and

The Past can Wait

placed on her lap, Maggie is offered the menu – the one without prices – and left to wait. The menu is in French. She recognises *escargots*, believes this is snails, and shudders.

If Luke wishes to make her feel comfortable in his rich bubble, this is not the way to go about it. She's made a mistake, agreeing to see him.

Anger trumps embarrassment. Before she loses courage, Maggie lifts the serviette from her lap and pushes back her chair. She will leave, explain to the haughty maître d' she is suddenly unwell … no, bugger explaining. She will simply leave.

Luke fills the space between her and escape. He is self-effacing, blustering apologies, a last-minute call from a fellow doctor, 'About our dear Mrs Harrington,' he says, sadness in his dark eyes. 'How could I not talk to him?'

Maggie sits, leaves the serviette on the table. Of course. She understands. Hiding her cowardice at wanting to leave, she agrees she herself would be late for God for Mrs Harrington. Luke's eyes brighten with glee at this forgiveness.

A bucket of ice appears by the table, a green, glistering champagne bottle burrowed into its depths.

A waiter smoothly pours a tasting amount for Luke, who sips, murmurs yes, and Maggie's wide, shallow glass is filled with golden fizziness, then Luke's. The waiter bows and backs away, his white linen towel neatly draped over his arm.

'To the future.' Luke raises his glass. 'You are particularly lovely this evening, Maggie.'

'To the future,' Maggie says, with little idea what she wishes it to be.

When the menu is perused, Maggie says yes to Luke's offer to choose for her. He has his own favourites here, he's sure Maggie will have never tasted anything like it, and Maggie laughs and tells Luke he is right, her familiarity with French food is sadly lacking. Luke says this needs to be fixed, it's the most divine cuisine in the world.

Maggie takes dainty mouthfuls of champagne and admires the knowledgeable way Luke discusses wines for their chosen courses with the sober-faced wine waiter – the sommelier, she learns, a separate and more illustrious being than the food waiter.

Her embarrassment submerged in champagne, Maggie decides this is what life is meant to be like. She listens to Luke's explanation about the chosen wine and decides she will ring June tomorrow. Poor June. Maggie's guilt at causing the caring June any sort of distress tarnishes her contentment. She will apologise for her outburst, tell her friend she has been right all along. Luke loves her.

Maggie's future emerges through the fizz of champagne to glitter at her fingertips, eager to be grasped.

◈◈◈◈◈

Anger – at Luke Elliott, not June – and the anticipation of humiliation on Maggie's behalf, churn Arthur's stomach. He rises from his chair, paces the room. He needs to run to Maggie, drag her from the edge of this disaster, tell her he's sorry for being an idiot and he loves her, loves her.

June is dialling. The phone trills at the other end of the line. A female voice answers.

'Mrs Greene? June here. I need to speak to Maggie, please.'

Mrs Greene chatters, excitement dancing through her incomprehensible words.

'Thanks, bye.' June replaces the handset. Her face is white.

'Maggie's out with Luke this evening,' she says. 'The reservation Enid overheard is definitely for Maggie and is for tonight. The best French restaurant in the city, Mrs Greene says. She's sure he's going to propose.'

'No. He's letting Maggie think he's going to propose,' Alf says, in an unconscious about turn. 'He's going to ditch her.'

Arthur's fury fills his throat. 'Which restaurant?'

June stares at him. 'Does it matter? She's there now. The best we can do is be here to comfort her when tomorrow comes.' She chews her bottom lip. 'Or congratulate her, if Mrs Greene is right.'

'Of course it matters.' Arthur can't wait until tomorrow. Either for congratulations or comfort. He's waited seven months. One more hour will kill him. The raw urge to speak to Maggie, plead forgiveness, tell her he wants them to be together, for all eternity, aches in his chest as deeply as the day after New Year.

'Which restaurant?' he asks again.

'Mrs Greene didn't know.'

Chapter Nineteen

'CAN'T BE TOO MANY FRENCH restaurants in the city,' Arthur says. His desperation makes him curt, demanding. 'Can there?' He will ring every one of them, a hundred if need be. Pay Alf's telephone bill for the rest of his years if it means he'll find Maggie.

Alf pulls a face. 'Not in the habit of frequenting pricey restaurants.'

June walks to the telephone table and pulls the directory from its shelf. 'Easiest way to find out.' She hands the thick book to Alf. 'You find restaurants and Arthur can ring.' She turns to Arthur. 'His surname is Elliott, for the reservation. I'll make tea in case this takes longer than it should.'

Alf sets the book on the coffee table and flips the pages. Arthur picks up the handset, finger poised ready to dial.

'R, r, r ...' Alf murmurs.

Arthur shifts from foot to foot. Every moment increases the urgency. What if this Dr Elliott is handing Maggie a giant glittering diamond as Alf finds R for restaurants? What if he's telling Maggie he no longer cares for her company and this is his farewell dinner? The first scenario is the worst. Maggie might let Arthur pick up the pieces if the second comes to pass. For her sake, he doesn't want that either.

'Here we go,' Alf says. 'Chez Noir, first on the list.'

Alf recites a number and Arthur dials, his finger too thick and heavy for the holes. The phone rings for an eternity until in another age, it's answered. Arthur gabbles his question and is curtly told, non, monsieur.

'Nope.' Arthur sets the receiver in its cradle with a clunk. 'Are there many?' How long is this going to take?

'Nah. Number two on the list–'

June bursts in, tea-less. 'Think I know which restaurant. There's one right by the hospital, very ritzy. Bet he's gone there.' She brings her clenched fist to her forehead, squeezes her eyes shut. 'What's its name?' she mutters. 'Not French, old-fashioned … damn this fuzzy pregnancy brain.'

Arthur and Alf share a frustrated look. Arthur is about to demand the second restaurant's number when June's face clears.

'Got it!' She beams.

'Yes?' Arthur and Alf shout together.

'The Quality Inn.'

'Sounds like a box of chocolates,' Alf grumbles. He traces the directory entries with his forefinger. 'Here we go,' he says, and reads out the numbers.

Arthur dials. A self-important voice with what Arthur is pretty sure is a fake French accent responds to his question with one of its own. 'Is there a problem? Might I take a message for le doctor?'

'No, no message, thanks.' Arthur hangs up. 'Thanks June, got him.'

'It's a few minutes' walk from the Royal,' June says, 'towards King William Road.'

'Right.' Arthur's on his way to the door. 'Hope I'm there in time.' If there's no bus, he'll run until he catches up with one.

June throws out her arms. 'We should have got the car back,' she says to Alf. 'No use to man or beast sitting at the repairers. You could have driven Arthur in.'

'No problem.' Alf slams shut the directory and jumps up. 'I'll take him on the bike. Got a spare leather jacket. It'll be a helluva lot quicker than any damn bus.'

◇◇◇◇◇

The oysters slip down Maggie's throat in a pleasing cool glide. The pale fish swimming in cream and topped with grapes is less tasty. Grapes? The champagne makes her bold enough to want to ask, teasingly, if this is the main course or pudding? Given the grave manner in which Luke chose their food, with frequent reference to the waiter for information on source and cooking method, Maggie holds the joke in. She is here to be impressed, and she determines to act out her role with the same level of gravity.

Luke talks about Mrs Harrington and how all they can do is keep her comfortable. Maggie's boldness melts into sadness. Death is a familiar acquaintance, of course. In this case, the old lady's quiet acceptance and her keen interest in the lesser problems of those around her have burrowed into Maggie's heart.

Laying his knife and fork at angles each side of his steak – so rare Maggie is reminded of an open wound in surgery – Luke wipes his mouth with the white linen serviette. 'Of course,' he says, with an arch of an eyebrow, 'the kindest thing would be to double her dose of morphine and have it done with, let her family have their lives back.'

'Pardon?' The word escapes Maggie's shocked mind before she can swallow it.

'You're a nurse. You must see how often it'd be best to let people go.' Luke's tone is amused indulgence.

Maggie bridles. She is reminded of her father's heart attack a little over a year ago. The doctors warned her mother, Teddy and herself, that he might never wake from the surgery. If he did, it was likely he would no longer be able to do what he had before taken for granted. Would Luke have allowed him to die? Although, Maggie admits, Mrs Harrington's case is different. The old lady is certainly dying. There might even be relief …

She cuts a piece of fish and puts it in her mouth to save answering. Luke doesn't pursue the conversation. He lightens the moment by moving on to his sister. He doesn't acknowledge Veronica's role in returning Maggie to his life. Instead, he quietly mocks her self-designated career as an interior designer.

'Mother and Father approve, for the time being.' He winks. 'Highly appropriate for a young lady as a means to pass her time until she marries.'

'Until she marries?'

'Why yes. Afterwards, she'll be busy with her home and

children.' The indulgent smile returns.

'Not every woman gives up work when they marry, not these days,' Maggie says. 'My sister-in-law and her sister run a thriving business, and both are married. One has children.'

'They are? She does?' His surprise seems genuine and Maggie wants to laugh. No, she won't. She is here to be impressed.

'They are and she does,' she says solemnly, placing her cutlery on the plate. 'And before you ask, their husbands support them all the way.' She doesn't add that in Raine's case, the money from the business pays the bulk of the household bills. A step too far.

'How lovely for them.' Luke's sardonic tone makes it apparent he finds this arrangement less than lovely.

Maggie takes in the implications. She wants her own home, and children. Does she want to give up her nursing? Possibly. If she does, it will be on her own terms, not because her husband expects it.

The champagne fizz dampens. Maggie's imagined glittering future tarnishes at the edges.

Luke lays his hand on hers. 'Let me say, to make it clear, any wife of mine would be able to make their own choices. I'm a modern man.'

His dancing eyes polish the tarnish to an acceptable gleam. Mostly.

The waiter pushes a wooden trolley to their table, laden with chocolate, pastry, and fruit wonders which send Maggie's taste buds quivering. She hasn't failed to notice many of the other women wave away this gilded carrier of wicked calories. Some do it with a languid lift of the hand, tolerant of the waiter's foolishness. As the evening and the volume of wine consumed gather pace, the younger women make a mocking fuss. They preen at the men's insistence they don't need to take care of their figures, they're far too perfect to worry about one dessert, and give in with a flirtatious pretence of reluctance.

Maggie knows her place. She is neither of these women. She points at a creamy custard with a toffee like topping, the simplest item on the trolley, and murmurs her thanks as the dish is laid before her with the reverence afforded a holy relic.

'You were talking about Veronica,' Maggie reminds Luke. She remembers the time in Veronica's smart flat, the young woman's hand squeezing her shoulder and the plea in her eyes. 'Why do you think she'll marry anyway?'

'Dear Veronica.' Glee lights Luke's face. 'The parents steer suitors in her direction on a regular basis. So far, my little sister has managed to avoid each and every one. Can't last. One day she'll fall in love, and that'll be that.'

'Hmm.' Sadly, Maggie also believes Veronica will fall in love one day, and if her family discover the unusual nature of that love, it will certainly be that. Does Luke truly have no idea?

The food and wine have done their job. Maggie is sated and impressed. Yet the contentment she held cupped in her open hands when the evening began – properly began with Luke's late and apologetic arrival – has proved fragile. She would like to recapture it, to have her mind and her heart reach out to the dancing eyes opposite her.

Luke returns her searching look. He smiles and Maggie smiles. When he reaches across the table, over the linen, around the candle glowing in its shallow holder, she puts her hands in his. They are warm, smooth, caressing. Welcoming hands. Maggie savours their touch.

'Maggie,' Luke says, 'I want to talk about us.'

◇◇◇◇◇

Arthur has forgotten the force of cold wind in his face, the way the sleeves of the leather jacket press against his arms as he is pressed against Alf's back. The roads are dry, the traffic light as they speed through the suburbs, leaning into the corners, Alf revving the engine at the rare red light and onto the main road into the city. Arthur is relieved to be moving, at last.

He tries to think what he will do when he gets to the restaurant, what he will say to Maggie, and to this doctor. A sense he is acting like a Victorian papa outraged at the suspected seduction of his virgin daughter niggles at his mind, mocking him. Maggie is old enough to make her own decisions, as she has amply pointed out. To marry whomever she wants to marry.

He ignores the niggle. Who cares if he acts ridiculous, storming in, demanding to know if the doctor's intentions are honourable? He's doing this for Maggie.

And for himself. He can't rely on secondhand tales, on the frailty of easy misunderstandings. He's relied on passed-on information for most of the last year, and it's led him deeper into heartache.

Alf takes a corner fast, and the bike leans a fraction too hard. Arthur automatically adjusts his weight, muscle memory taking over from the many, many times he has ridden with Alf. The bike rights itself, smoothly, and Alf accelerates along a straight stretch and into King William Road. They pass a tram trundling along the middle of the road, its passengers gazing out of windows or staring into newspapers. They wait at a red light, and turn into North Terrace.

Alf slows. Arthur peers at the signs.

He taps Alf's shoulder. 'There,' and points a short way ahead at the discreet sign, The Quality Inn.

Alf pulls into the curb, at right angles between two parked cars. One is a long-bonneted Chrysler coupe, with a doctor's sign in the window allowing the driver to park wherever he wishes. Arthur scowls, dismounts, and unzips the borrowed jacket to hand it to Alf.

'Don't be stupid,' Alf says. 'Keep it on. Cold enough to freeze the whatsits off a brass monkey, in case you haven't noticed.' He kicks out the bike's stand, remains seated. 'Do you want me to wait?'

'No.' That would be an admission of failure. 'Thanks, Alf. You're a true pal. You and June.'

'June's upset, worries she's done the wrong thing, encouraging Maggie with this guy.'

Arthur agrees. For selfish reasons, he hopes with his whole heart June has been wrong the entire time. He also, if he works hard to be fair, can admit June's been supporting her friend the best way she knows.

He says, 'Tell June not to fret. Bad for the baby.' He grimaces. 'Besides, she might have been right all along. Maggie and this Luke guy could be a match made in heaven.' The words, spoken out loud, tear at his gut.

He rezips the jacket. 'Talk to you tomorrow.' And walks towards the sign.

⬥⬥⬥⬥⬥

'Talk about us?' Maggie returns Luke's look, keeping her hands in his. Her heart pumps hard. 'What about us?' It's hard to keep her tone light when her emotions are tangled in a knotted cluster beneath her breastbone. She has no idea what she wants Luke to say.

'Yes.' Luke lowers their joined hands to the linen cloth. Candlelight plays on his strong jaw, his straight nose, reflects in his brown eyes, making them hard to read. 'We've had what you might call a stormy time over the past few months, haven't we?'

Like his eyes, his tone is hard to read. All Maggie hears is that he is serious.

'You could say so.' Her lips curve into a smile meant to denote agreement, hinting a touch of shame at having been the source of the storm. Does she feel shame? She would search for it, to see, except Luke is talking, his voice as smooth as the creamy dessert Maggie has recently enjoyed.

'I've been persistent though, haven't I?' He nods, prompting her confession before he will continue with whatever is on his mind.

Maggie obliges. 'You have, Luke.'

'Patient,' he adds, his candlelit eyes peering into hers.
'Most patient.' Maggie laughs.

◇◇◇◇◇

Arthur itches to lift the false French poser from the too-thick carpet and deposit him onto the pavement, into the cold.

No, Monsieur cannot enter without a tie – with a sneering glance at the scarred leather jacket – and what is urgent enough he must interrupt le doctor's meal? Especially – the man raises a thin, groomed eyebrow – at this point in the evening. Is it a matter of life and death?

This point in the evening? Arthur squints into the yellow gloom of the restaurant, his gaze roving from one table to the next.

He finds her in a far corner. Maggie, beautiful in a red top and colourful scarf, her black curls pinned up in a sophisticated style. Her hair, and her thinner face, make her appear more elegant than the Maggie of seven months ago. She and her companion hold hands across the table. Maggie's head is lifted, laughing her wide-mouthed laugh. She gazes into the man's eyes, her whole self concentrating on this one person. She is glorious.

She is in love. Clear as day.

Arthur's chest tightens. His lungs refuse to either take in or expel air. The force of his need to see her, to save her if need be, the energy which has brought him here, leaks from his body with a rushed whoosh, like air from a blown tyre.

The Frenchman is muttering where is the emergency, and Monsieur must leave. He places a firm hand on the despised leather sleeve and steers Arthur around to face the door.

Arthur doesn't resist. His body is empty of emotion. His head, heart and soul are a void.

June has been right all along.

He is too late. This elegant Maggie who dines with rich, handsome men in French restaurants has moved beyond him. He will be glad for her. He will.

Arthur shrugs his arm from the poser's hold. He turns from the living golden glow of the restaurant and slowly walks into the night.

⋄⋄⋄⋄⋄

Maggie laughs, and lifts her head.

The laughter stills in her throat. She frowns. By the lectern which holds the reservation book, a man in a shabby leather jacket is being turned away by the maître d'.

Her pulse jumps. It can't be? How on earth? Maggie squints through the low light. She can hear her own heart.

The man – it's Arthur, she would know him anywhere – shakes off the Frenchman's hold on his arm and walks slowly to the door. He pushes it open. A brief glimpse of streetlights, the rattle of a tram, a car horn, and he is through, closing the door quietly after him.

'Maggie, what is it?' Luke has taken his hands from hers. He peers at her, then over his shoulder to the entrance.

There's nothing to see. Arthur is gone.

A waiter walks towards them, hands Maggie a slip of paper, murmurs something about a Mrs Hall and a message.

Maggie glances at it, and returns her gaze to Luke. His brow is furrowed, his gorgeous eyes inviting her.

One thought loops in Maggie's mind. June's words, the day Maggie learned of Arthur's marriage.

And he's here. Waiting for you.

She smiles at Luke. She knows what she wants to happen.

Chapter Twenty

IF HER MOTHER TRIES TO adjust Maggie's long veil one more time, she will rip it from her head and refuse to wear the damn thing.

'Leave it, Mum, please, for God's sake.' She pushes Nancy's hand away with what remains of her patience. 'Shouldn't you have left already?'

Nancy glances at her watch and gasps. 'Yes, yes, I should have. Need to make sure your dad is ready … ' She twists about, searching the small room in case her husband is hiding in a corner. 'Where has he gotten to?'

'He's in the living room with Raine and Teddy.' June steers the flustered mother-of-the-bride to the door, opens it, and urges Nancy into the passage. 'We'll see you at the church.'

'The church.' Nancy breathes her smug satisfaction. 'A proper wedding this time.' She scurries along the short passageway, high heels beating a soft tattoo on the carpet runner.

June closes the door and laughs. 'I wish I could have been here when your brother and Raine were married. Must have been hilarious.'

Maggie snorts. 'Hilarious isn't the word I'd use. Everyone pretending Raine wasn't in the family way.' She grins at the phrase. 'Mum will never forgive her for leading her golden boy astray.' She returns her gaze to the mirror. 'Everything's dandy these days, thank God. Two grandkids make up for a lot.'

Standing from the dressing table stool, Maggie leans into the mirror to check her lipstick. Her cheeks are fuller. Happiness is filling out the sharp planes and bony angles of her winter of uncertainty, as she thinks of it. Her appetite has returned, and she's glad.

'Right, think I'm ready to face the music.' Turning to June, she admires the way her friend's figure has returned to its previous slimness after the birth of baby Deborah. As their friendship has returned to the closeness of before, with all explained and forgiven.

June's blue, boat-necked satin dress accents her eyes, as do the blue flowers sitting in her blonde curls. 'You're a stunner, Mrs Hall. How about me? Will I pass, matron-of-honour?'

'Oh yes! Beautiful.' June claps her hands together, eyeing Maggie from veil to satin shoes. 'We did well, picking your gown.'

'Agreed.' Maggie runs her hands lightly over the fitted bodice with its lace overlay and three quarter length lace sleeves. The creamy heavy satin skirt balloons a short way from a tight waist before curving in towards the ankles. A gown for a princess.

The thought takes her fleetingly to the party at Luke's house not quite a year ago. To the time when her mother's unusual good taste in a dress had Maggie thinking of herself as Cinderella off to the ball, to dance the night away with her Prince Charming. She smiles at the memory.

'Let's find Veronica, shall we, and hope the groom is on time?'

'Veronica's with Jenny and Stevie, helping Raine make sure your niece and nephew are fully prepared for their parts.' June tugs gently at Maggie's veil. 'Brave of you to have the two little ones as part of the show.'

'They're great kids. And I don't care,' Maggie says, 'if they act up, although not too much. It'll distract people from me.'

It's never been all about the wedding itself for Maggie, although she intends to have fun playing queen for a day. No. The future is what has always excited her, and now her new life beckons, with its planned pleasures. First, the house. They'll move in immediately after their honeymoon in New Zealand. Maggie has spent many joyous hours choosing furniture, rugs, curtains and making the place

The Past can Wait

homely and comfortable. Proper chairs to curl up in with a book, none of this hard-angled nonsense.

A knock on the door, and Veronica pokes her pixie head into the room. 'Come on, ladies, the world and his dog are waiting for you.' She squints at Maggie. 'Not changed your mind, have you? Don't think I could stand it.'

Maggie walks to the door, pulls it open, and draws her young friend into a silk and lace hug. 'No way,' she whispers. 'Still okay?'

'Yes, yes. I approve!'

Veronica leads the way out of the house and into the garden. The autumn sun shines strongly, putting its blessing on the day. The bridal cars, complete with white ribbons, are lined up on the road. Neighbours gather to watch, and wave, and cheer. Her father stands by one, the door open, waiting for the bride.

Maggie pauses on the gravelled path, halfway between the porch and the iron gate. Mindful of her veil, she shifts to face the house. 'Goodbye, home,' she murmurs. 'After today, I'll be a visitor. You make sure you look after Mum and Dad, all right?' She blows the house a kiss, and walks sedately to the car. Her heart might burst.

◇◇◇◇◇

The groom shifts from foot to foot, his nerves strung taut. Is it like this for every man about to be married?

Whispers, discreet coughs and the shuffling of women's carefully chosen best outfits and men's brushed suits reach his ears. The church is filling, the guests sliding along the dark pews marked with a white horseshoe and spray of red and white roses.

Is it time yet? Is the wait over?

'How much longer?' he whispers to his best man, grave and silent beside him. He's grateful for the calming presence.

'Not long now.' The best man wriggles his shoulders in their close fitting morning jacket.

Not long.

As if magicked by the words, the organist strikes up 'Here Comes the Bride'.

The groom raises his eyebrows at the solemn best man. Maggie the traditionalist. His teasing about choosing this tune fell on deaf ears. She was adamant.

'I want to shout to the world, we're marrying, I'm a bride.' Maggie's eyes glistened with self-mocking humour. She meant it, though.

He swings about to face the congregation, which has stood, every eye on the wide church doorway. He has the best view.

First in the parade is Veronica, her short chestnut hair glowing, her smile broad. Behind her, Jenny and Stevie's eyes are glued to Veronica's back in the certain knowledge that moving their heads an inch to left or right will bring the church collapsing in a pile of rubble. June walks next, a motherly eye on the children.

The groom strains to peer past them, anxious right up to the wire. The doorway remains empty for a long heartbeat, two … and she is there, carrying her bouquet of roses, her arm in Mr Greene's who stands tall and proud beside his beautiful daughter.

Maggie is here, really here. She walks towards him, her veil trailing from her shiny black curls. She gives tiny waves to the guests on either side, as gracious as a queen. He can feel his lips stretching into a beatific smile, keeping his gaze on her face.

She is as gorgeous, as elegant, as she was the night in the French restaurant. His chest is too small for his heart. He hears it pattering, punching at his ribs like a boxer in a ring. She reaches the front. He takes her hand as her father lifts her fingers from his arm and, with a stern arch of his eyebrows, moves to his seat in the pews.

Maggie's dark eyes meet his. The corners of her mouth lift and his heart might burst.

She has come to him.

The Past can Wait

She has come to him just like she came to him that freezing winter night, running coatless, heels clicking on the wide pavement slabs of the Terrace, calling.

'Arthur! Arthur!'

He swivelled about, disbelief and joy mingling in his pounding heart.

Maggie threw herself against him, crying, laughing, vowing to never again, ever, let him go.

Standing before the priest, a keener joy surges through Arthur's body. He takes Maggie's hand, slips on the ring. He vows he will never again, ever, let her go.

Thank you for reading

Thank you for reading *The Past can Wait*. It was never my intention to write one sequel to *Keepers,* let alone two of what I now call spin-offs. However, the way in which the first spin-off, *Walking in the Rain*, was so warmly welcomed by fans of *Keepers* led to book three.

The challenge once again was to write a book which could also be read as a standalone, and I hope I've done this. Maggie and Arthur have been solid secondary characters up until now, and it was high time they got their own story. It was a pleasure to bring Libby back into the tale too, and give her a much deserved happy ever after.

… and please leave a review

If *The Past can Wait* has given you an enjoyable moment of romantic escapism, I would be very grateful if you took a little time to write a review, or even just leave a rating – that's fine too – on Amazon, Goodreads or BookBub.

We indie authors don't have the resources of publishing houses behind us to promote our books and we rely heavily on reviews and word-of-mouth recommendations from satisfied readers to spread the word.

Do note that you don't need to have purchased the book from Amazon in order to leave a review.

Other brilliant ways to help are to tell a friend, post how much you enjoyed the book on social media, recommend *The Past can Wait* to your book club, ask your local library to get it in.

Thank you so much for your support!

If you haven't read *Keepers* or *Walking in the Rain*, learn more about them on the following pages.

Cheryl
April 2024

Keepers

A US Amazon bestseller in Australian Historical Fiction for several months, Raine, Teddy and Alf's story has proved popular with readers, with comments such as

> *A heartwarming historical fiction that I could read again and again.*
>
> *I loved the characters and the story grabs you and won't let go until the last page.*
>
> *A story that slowly took hold and you could not stop reading until the end when you discovered it was 3 in the morning!*

At eight months pregnant, Raine shouldn't be on a jolting bus crawling through snow searching for her husband. He might not want to be found. She might not want to find him.

It's 1951, Australia, and while Raine's marriage to the good looking but moody Teddy was unplanned, all seems well despite their uncertain start. Cash is short, but their baby thrives and they get by. Then Teddy disappears, sending a telegram which may or may not be the reason for his desertion. Grieving and furious in equal measure, Raine's struggles to cope are made harder when she realises she's carrying their second child.

Her willing helpmate is the faithful, devoted Alf - Teddy's best friend since their wartime Cockney childhood. He's always looked out for Raine. He'd love to do so forever, he tells her. Has Raine given her heart to the wrong man?

When Teddy is found, his reluctance to return forces Raine to act. With an unwilling Alf beside her, she sets out on a punishing journey to track her husband down. She needs to look him in the eye. She needs to discover the truth of their love.

Find *Keepers* on Amazon.

Walking in the Rain

Keen to discover what happens next, many readers have followed up *Keepers* with this novella sequel, and found it equally engrossing –

Although I was going to read it slowly, I finished it in one day.

The book is as endearing and heartwarming as the first novel.

I made the fatal mistake of thinking I would read a couple of chapters before going to bed. I found myself unable to go to bed until I finished the whole thing.

Once, Alf's bruised heart let love slip by. Now he's ready, but is he too late?

1954, Australia. Three years ago in a hospital in the Snowy Mountains, Alf stood by while the woman he loved reunited with her wayward husband. These days, Raine and Teddy are his best friends, their children call him Uncle Alf.

Now Alf stands by as his days slip into loveless tedium. June, a nurse, witnessed the anguish in Alf's eyes. A spark flared between them. A tentative kiss was exchanged. But Alf's heart wasn't ready. Life moved on.

Pushed into searching for a new start, Alf returns to the mountains. He tells himself finding June isn't the reason he's there. Which is probably for the best, because it seems June has already found the man of her dreams.

Can the stars be made to align this time? Or will life move on again?

Find *Walking in the Rain* on Amazon.

Acknowledgments

Many thanks once again to my critique partners, Jodi and Paula, for living with this book for many months and reading it more than once. Couldn't do this without you. Also thank you to those members of Dean Writers Circle who gave constructive help during the early drafting. And to superfan Averil for her valuable beta feedback.

Finally, my loving thanks to my patient, tolerant husband, David Harris, without whom this book would not exist.

Any spelling, grammatical or design flaws are entirely my own.

Cheryl Burman grew up as the child forever reading on her bed. But as this was Australia, she was also often tempted outside to the beach and the yabby creeks near her suburban home. When she moved to the Forest of Dean, UK, she followed the likes of Tolkien, Rowling and many others in being inspired to write. As a devout Narnia fan, she started with middle grade fantasy, discovered a taste for historical fiction, and then combined the two into historical fantasy.

Given she is lucky enough to live in a place chock-a-block full of history, legend and myth, there is much to draw on. She does so, as well as on her own childhood in Australia.

Two of her novels have won awards, as have several of her flash fiction pieces and short stories. Some of these are included in her two short story collections, while others are published in various anthologies.

A keen student of writing craft, Cheryl has had articles published on writing-related topics both online and in print, and maintains a popular writing tips post on her blog.

As Cheryl Mayo, she is a former chair of Dean Writers Circle and a founder of Dean Scribblers, which encourages creative writing among young people in her community.

All her books, including purchase links, can be found on her website.

Printed in Great Britain
by Amazon